Back to the Dark Ages!

Richard Sloane

Order this book online at www.trafford.com
or email orders@trafford.com

Most Trafford titles are also available at major online book retailers.

Printed in the United States of America.

ISBN: 978-1-4669-7399-2 (sc)
ISBN: 978-1-4669-7401-2 (hc)
ISBN: 978-1-4669-7400-5 (e)

Library of Congress Control Number: 2012924041

Trafford rev. 02/05/2013

 www.trafford.com

North America & international
toll-free: 1 888 232 4444 (USA & Canada)
phone: 250 383 6864 ♦ fax: 812 355 4082

Chapter 1

My name is June and I am now 21 although the adventure I'm going to describe happened when I was eleven. But I remember it as if it was yesterday. At that time my best friend was a boy called August who I called Augie and who was the same age as me and in the same class at our local primary school. His birthday was in August and his family originally American and these two reasons, he told me, accounted for his strange name. We were living practically next door to each other and were thrown together because we were the only two children we knew who were both named after months of the year. We had a lot in common, including our love of music and reading. He played the recorder and I sang in a choir and played the piano. We often lent our story books to each other and grew up wanting intensely to have an adventure like those we had read about. But we never dreamed we would actually have one.

We lived in a quiet seaside town on the East coast of England and our parents gave us lots of freedom. So in autumn and spring we often used to fly our kites together on the beach while in summer we would go paddling in the sea. Everyone knew us in the town and, as long as we were together, our parents did not mind us going out alone without an adult to accompany us. But of course we had to be home by a particular time.

Then, one day in summer, a funfair came to town. Neither of us had ever been to a real funfair. We were used only to the ice cream sellers and donkeys which used to appear, as if by magic, as soon as the weather turned warm. Naturally we were very excited at the prospect of visiting it and keen to see what it had to offer. So one Tuesday afternoon after school we were given some money by our parents and told to be back by suppertime.

We rushed together down to the pier where the fair was being held and, as we approached, we were amazed to see all the activity going on in and around it. We had never seen anything so exciting before in our little town. We had decided before we left that we would walk around and see what we wanted to do before spending our precious money. So we went in and were immediately dazed by the din and the lights. The noise seemed to be coming from all sides, from slot machines spitting out sweets to the rides which all had massive loudspeakers attached to them blaring out music or calling the people to try them. Also it was packed. We saw a lot of our school friends running around like maniacs, many of them eating candy floss on big sticks and getting the sweet, sticky sugar all over their faces.

We walked around for a while, confused and disoriented until, finally, on the far side of the fair, we saw an unoccupied bench on which to sit. So we sat down and looked around. Then Augie spotted what appeared to be a large carousel tucked away behind the other rides. 'That looks like fun,' he said and I agreed. So we walked over in its direction.

As we got closer, the din of the funfair seemed to fade away and, when we came right up to it, all the noise had completely disappeared and we seemed to be enclosed in a bubble of pure blessed silence. We could now see that there were some words engraved around the carousel which said, 'Let the magic carousel take you on the adventure of a lifetime!' The horses all looked new and almost perfectly real. They were many different shades of black, brown and white while some were piebald and the predominant colours of the carousel itself were red and gold. It looked to our young eyes, well, 'magical' is the only word I can think of. It was spinning madly, all its horses going up and down in unison, but there seemed to be nobody on it. This surprised us but pleased us too as we thought we might be able to have the whole thing to ourselves and it looked like the funnest thing in the whole fair.

We went up to an old man sitting in a booth who seemed to be operating it. He was wearing a full clown costume with a painted face so that the only part of **him** you could see was a pair of strange purple-coloured eyes behind the paint. 'Can we have a go,' Augie asked.

'By all means, children,' he replied in an unusually high, squeaky kind of voice. 'Go around and choose your horses.'

'How much is it?' I asked, fearing that we might not have enough money. But the funny old man simply laughed and said, 'Pay me when you get off if you think it's worth it.' And he pulled a lever. The carousel shuddered to a halt but nobody got off.

So we walked around it, inspecting the horses carefully. They all had names attached to their bridles, some of which we recognised: Pegasus, Shadowfax, Whirlwind, Black Beauty, Silver, and many others with strange-sounding names which we couldn't pronounce. We finally decided on Pegasus for me, a gorgeous white beast with a golden harness (but, unfortunately, I remember thinking, without wings) and Black Beauty for August which was right next to it on the carousel and was indeed a most beautiful animal.

'Good choices, children,' the old man called out from his booth. We were, strangely, still alone as we climbed onto our horses. Then he set the carousel in motion and we started spinning around.

Chapter 2

Weirdly, however, we seemed to be spinning **backwards**. We didn't get dizzy, which surprised me, but I held out my hand and August took it. I think it made us feel safer holding hands. With our other hands we gripped the reins of our horses tightly and the carousel just kept spinning faster and faster. But strangely we felt no harm could come to us.

Then with a mighty crash we seemed to be propelled right through some kind of barrier and we suddenly came back to earth, landing as softly as two feathers. Our metal horses had somehow been transformed into real horses! They still had their names attached to their bridles and we could feel their soft flanks heaving with their quiet breathing.

We looked around but nothing seemed familiar. There was no sign of the funfair. Indeed there was no sign of life at all. We seemed to be in a large clearing in a forest. We could see only tall trees all around us but there was soft grass underneath.

'What happened?' I asked Augie.

'I've no idea,' he replied. 'Where are we?' But that too was unanswerable for the moment.

But I still wasn't scared, just in a state of wonderment. It was like being thrown back into a fairy tale.

Then Augie said, 'We wanted an adventure, didn't we?' I nodded and he went on, 'Well, now we seem to be in the middle of one.'

I nodded again and said, 'What now though?' but Augie just shrugged.

Then suddenly everything changed. Our horses pricked up their ears and started cantering across the clearing. Neither of us had ever ridden a real horse in our lives, only the donkeys on the beach, but we soon got the hang of it. The only problem was that we seemed to be unable either to steer the horses or stop them. They were much too powerful for us to control. But they appeared to know where they were going and we were soon galloping down forest tracks hanging on for dear life, Black Beauty leading and Pegasus following.

When we finally emerged from the forest, we found ourselves in open country with the sea glittering in the distance. Then we saw our first signs of human habitation. Little thatched wooden huts were scattered across the plain like pieces on a chess board. Only there seemed to be no rhyme or reason for where they were placed. There was nothing remotely familiar to us and we still hadn't seen a single human being.

The horses had stopped and now they turned their great heads to look at us as if they were watching over us. We patted their necks to reassure them and they suddenly took off like bullets from a gun. We could do nothing but go along for the ride and were galloping now at a furious pace across the open plain. It seemed to us as if we had been riding for ever but we didn't feel tired or saddle-sore, just immensely excited to find out where the horses were taking us. We were in a state of total exhilaration.

The next thing we knew we were heading straight through a small village and here we saw our first people. They were small, brown and mostly barefoot and seemed to be dressed in old rags. They were very surprised to see us on our powerful horses and scattered out of the way of their hooves. A couple of the people called out after us but we didn't understand what they were saying, perhaps because of the noise of the wind we were making or of the thudding of the hooves on the ground. Then the village was behind us and we were in open countryside again. We seemed to be heading roughly in the direction of the sea and I leant over to Augie, who was riding next to me, pointed and shouted, 'We should recognise something once we get to the sea.' He looked dubious but then nodded and shouted back, 'I hope so, June.'

The horses dashed on, apparently inexhaustible, and we saw that we were now riding parallel to the sea. Then we came to the mouth of a great river and followed it along its bank until we saw rising out of the heat haze our first proper building not far ahead. But, instead of heading straight for it, our horses turned and made for a small wood nearby. They had slowed to a canter by now and soon it was a trot as we approached the wood. They obviously knew a way through it because they found a path easily to its centre and we soon came out into a sunlit clearing with a small stream running through it. There we saw an old man, dressed in what looked like monk's robes, kneeling on the ground and obviously praying in front of a small pile of stones with a cross on top. Next to him stood an old brown mare, quietly grazing on the grass. Pegasus and Black Beauty went up to the old horse and nuzzled her affectionately. She clearly knew them and nuzzled them back and then the three horses all started grazing contentedly.

Knowing this must be the end of the road, we slipped off our horses and walked over to the old man, holding hands, not knowing what to expect, but still feeling that no harm could come to us in this peaceful place. We were beyond wonderment now. He raised his head, which was covered by a monk's hood, and looked at us. He had kindly eyes and we immediately trusted him, especially as we knew that our horses, which we also trusted implicitly, wouldn't have taken us to a place of danger. Then, getting up from his praying position, he spoke.

Chapter 3

However, what he said was in such strange English that we didn't immediately understand him. He repeated his question and this time we got it. He was asking us our names.

I said, 'My name's June and this is my friend, August.'

'June and August,' he mused, savouring the sound of the syllables. Then he asked us something else but this time we didn't understand him at all. He had to repeat the question three times, each time more slowly than the last, before we understood. He was asking us where we came from. He had not only kind eyes but a soft, gentle voice which we liked.

This time it was Augie who replied, 'We come from Eastport. Where are we, sir, if I may ask?'

'Eastport? Really?' the old man said. Then, after a pause, he said, 'You are near Jarrow.'

I knew where Jarrow was as I had a cousin who lived in Newcastle we used to visit occasionally. I burst out, 'But that's miles from Eastport!'

He just nodded and then Augie asked, 'What is your name please, sir?'

'You can call me Father Bede,' he replied.

Then I made a connection with what we had seen so far which hit me like a bolt of lightning. 'And what year is it please, Father Bede?' I asked.

'It's the year of our Lord 731,' he replied.

I turned to Augie and said wonderingly, 'We've been thrown backwards in time! We are in the Dark Ages!'

He replied anxiously, 'It seems that way.' Then, after a moment's reflection, he added, 'What will our parents do if we're not back by suppertime?'

I hadn't thought of that and turned back to Father Bede who seemed to have understood the question. He looked deep into our eyes and then at our horses and said, 'Don't worry about that, June and August. Your horses will have you back by suppertime.' And now some sort of translation switch must have been thrown in our brains because we understood him perfectly, and we believed him. Then, walking between us, lightly holding each of us by the elbow, he led us back to our horses, saying, 'Come. We will return to my monastery.'

So we all mounted after Pegasus and Black Beauty had knelt down to help us get up onto their high backs. Then we walked slowly back to the large building we had seen earlier. It was made mostly of wood but the church at its centre was stone. My head was buzzing with so many questions I didn't know where to start and I knew Augie's would be too. But Father Bede seemed to be lost in thought and neither of us dared to ask anything. So we rode in silence. I suspected that Father Bede would have many questions to ask us too but then it was almost like he had been expecting us so maybe not. I was amazed at first that he hadn't been more surprised at the sudden arrival of two children from the future but back then I couldn't have known what I was to find out later.

We went into the monastery through a great door which opened wide to let us pass and then we were in a sort of courtyard with many other monks and what must have been country people scurrying around on their business. A short monk came running up to Father Bede and helped him dismount. He looked curiously at us and our patron bade him to help us down from our huge animals. He did this and then led all three horses away, presumably to the stables. Father Bede said, 'Follow me,' and he led us to the kitchen which was a hive of activity. Servants were cooking great sides of meat on spits while others were clanking around with saucepans. The noise and the heat reminded me a little of the funfair and I wondered how much weirder things could get.

There the good Father introduced us to a stout lady who seemed to be in charge. He called her Sister Ethelreda and asked her to find us some more appropriate clothes than the jeans, T-shirts and trainers we were wearing, which were attracting strange looks from everybody in the kitchen, and then to bring us to him in his study. She took us behind the kitchen to what must have been the servants' quarters and what I remember most vividly about them was the smell which seemed to hang in the air like a blanket. It wasn't a disgusting smell by any means but it was certainly the smell of people who weren't used to having a shower every evening like us. Sister Ethelreda saw us wrinkling our noses and asked in a kind voice where we were from. We couldn't tell her we came from the future so I just said we came from a different far-away country and she seemed to accept this.

She went over to a corner of the small room we were in to a large wooden chest and drew out two tunics made of some kind of rough cloth which she held up against us to make sure they fitted. Then she asked us to undress and put them on. I looked at Augie and he blushed but I just said, 'We have to forget all our old ideas while we're here. Don't be embarrassed.' While we were getting undressed, I saw her looking at our almost naked bodies and almost asked her to stop staring until I remembered that, with our strange clothes, to her we must have looked like a couple of aliens from a distant planet. We were both pale-skinned and I had masses of blonde hair done in a ponytail with a rubber band while Augie had flaming red hair and was covered in freckles. I was quite tall for my age and Augie was a bit shorter than me but stocky.

Anyway, we did as she asked, taking off everything including our trainers except our underclothes, and put on the tunics which felt rough to our delicate skins but at least were clean and smelled fresh—not with the freshness of our fabric conditioners at home but a natural kind of freshness like spring water. Then she gave us a pair of sandals each and we put them on our bare feet. We felt very free in our new clothes and I felt like dancing for joy. The Sister saw us smiling at each other and she smiled too, saying when we had finished dressing, 'That's much better. You could almost pass for two of us now.'

Then she took us back through the kitchen again to the main part of the monastery. We came to a small oak door which she knocked on and we were invited inside by Father Bede's soft voice.

Chapter 4

He looked us up and down approvingly and then thanked Sister Ethelreda who left the room. He bade us make ourselves comfortable on a pile of soft cushions scattered on the floor and we looked around. The room itself was sparsely furnished but there were piles of papers everywhere, giving it rather a cluttered look. He was sitting behind a large wooden table with quills and pieces of parchment on it, all covered with writing. Then, when we had sat down, he spoke.

'So you two have come from the future to help us. Is that right?'

'We know nothing about helping you. But, yes, it seems as though we are back in your time,' I said.

'Which century do you come from, pray?' he asked.

Augie replied proudly, 'The twenty first century. But how did we get here?'

'The twenty first century,' he said in wonder. Then he added, 'I prayed for somebody to come but, to be honest, I never expected two children.'

'You prayed for us to come,' I asked in disbelief.

'No, not you specifically. Just anybody. And now my prayers have been answered.'

'But we never asked to come here!' Augie burst out.

'No, but now you are here, you can help us.'

'How?' I asked

'I'll tell you later.' And we had to be content with that. Now he changed the subject. 'Would you like to see your horses?' he asked.

'Yes, please!' we both said in unison, forgetting for the moment the help which we were supposed to be providing him with. I think we felt that only our horses could keep us anchored somehow to reality as some sort of reminder of our former lives.

So we followed him out of his study, back out of the monastery and round its side to some wooden stables. There we were greeted by the sight of our two gorgeous animals which had clearly been groomed. They stood there positively gleaming in the late afternoon sunlight, one pure black and the other a glorious shade of milky white. They whinnied softly when they saw us and we went up to them and stroked their huge necks and flanks. Father Bede said, 'They are the best I have ever seen. I wonder how my old mare knew them. Ah well, just another miracle probably.'

I looked at Augie and whispered, 'Of course! That's why he wasn't surprised by us coming from the future. He believes in miracles!' I don't know if Father Bede heard me or not but he just ignored this comment. Augie, however, nodded and we continued patting the horses and then looked around the stables more closely. There were several other horses in them, none as beautiful as ours though, and a lot of riding equipment, harnesses, saddles and suchlike. They smelled of horse dung and horse sweat. I said to Augie, 'I bet stables haven't changed much in the last 1500 years.'

'It's true,' he replied. 'I went to some stables once on a school trip and they were pretty similar to these. Smelled the same too.'

'Good,' said Father Bede. 'That is what I was hoping for. To show you that things don't actually change much over time. Now come along. It's suppertime.'

Augie looked at Father Bede and said, 'You promised us we would be home for supper.'

'And so you will, children, **your** suppertime. But time means something completely different now that you have travelled through it. You can stay here as long as you want and I will still have you home in time. Your parents won't miss you, I promise. And you won't get any older, just wiser, maybe.' Father Bede spoke with such assurance and certainty that we both took him at his word and were actually relieved that the adventure we were on would not end too quickly.

'OK,' Augie said although, because he spoke in old English, he did not actually say 'OK' but that was the meaning. 'I believe you. I'm happy we can stay longer with you.'

'So am I!' I agreed enthusiastically.

Then we turned and with a last look at the horses, followed Father Bede back to the main part of the monastery where we went into a large room with a high ceiling, lit by many candles. It was full of monks all sitting in rows on wooden benches silently contemplating the empty bowls, spoons and wooden cups in front of them on the tables. As soon as Father Bede entered, however, they all stood up and bowed their heads as we passed through them and up to a table, set on a kind of platform at the end of the room. He placed us one on either side of him and then said

Grace in Latin. We understood just enough of it to know that that was what he was doing.

When he had finished, he raised his head and said to the assembled monks, 'Dear ones, we have today to greet and welcome as our own two very special strangers who have travelled far to be with us in this, our time of need. This is August and this is June.'

'August and June,' the assembled monks said, trying to get their tongues around the unfamiliar sounds. We bowed to them as they had done to us before.

'I wish you all to accord them the highest degree of hospitality. Thank you.' And with that he sat down and signalled to the servants standing around the walls to begin serving the food. Some turned to several large crockery pots or tureens, as I learnt to call them later in life, which had appeared during Grace, and began ladling out a kind of stew into the empty bowls. Others went around with big jugs of water filling up our empty cups. The stew was giving off the most fantastic aroma and we tried it and found that it was indeed delicious. There were bits of meat in it and lots of vegetables and herbs and we suddenly realised how hungry we were. We ate with relish and had seconds when they were offered. At the end of the meal, which to our surprise was held in silence, Father Bede stood up again and said, 'Now let us pray.' And everyone stood and offered up a silent prayer of thanks for the meal. Then Father Bede left the room with us following and all the other monks filing out behind us.

Sister Ethelreda was waiting for us outside and Father Bede put us into her care saying, 'You two need to rest now. Go with the Sister and sleep well. We will talk again tomorrow.' And with those words he left. Sister Ethelreda then led us back to the same servants' quarters we had dressed in earlier where we found our modern clothes neatly folded and lying on the big oak chest. Two straw beds with warm-looking blankets on them had appeared and, after showing us where the chamber pots were kept in a tiny cupboard, which shocked us a bit, the Sister left us alone. We were too tired now to talk about our extraordinary day so we just lay down without even taking our clothes off and fell asleep almost immediately.

Chapter 5

That night we slept well as our straw beds were surprisingly comfortable and woke with the sunrise feeling refreshed. However, we were both amazed that we were still back in the old times and that it hadn't all been a fantastic dream. Having washed as best we could in the bucket of cold water we had been given, we were ready to talk.

'One thing's for sure,' Augie said, 'I'm going to need a decent bath when I get home.'

I grinned and said, 'Yes, but before that we have to continue our adventure. Perhaps we should make a list of questions for Father Bede.'

'OK, starting with how we are supposed to be able to help him,' Augie said.

'True,' I replied. 'What else do you want to ask? All the questions I had when we first met him seem to have gone completely out of my head.'

'Mine too.' Augie said. 'Maybe we are getting used to being here.'

At that moment Sister Ethelreda appeared, looking exactly as she had done the day before, and said, 'Come on then, children. It's breakfast time.'

'Oh, good,' Augie said. 'I'm hungry.'

'I'm afraid he's always hungry,' I said apologetically.

'That's good,' she said. 'I'm glad he's got a decent appetite. He's still growing after all.'

Then we followed her, not this time to the great dining hall but back to the kitchen which we found, like yesterday, buzzing with activity. She sat us down at one of the long tables there and we ate delicious home-made bread with some kind of lovely jam washed down with big cups of fresh, creamy milk. Nobody there paid much attention to us but they seemed to be in some awe of us as we noticed some sideways glances which immediately turned away back to what they were doing when they saw us looking back at them. I realised then that we still hadn't seen any children in the monastery and this made me feel a bit sad.

When we had finished, Sister Ethelreda took us back to Father Bede's study. He was there writing and looked up as we entered. 'Come in, August and June,' he said welcomingly. So we went in and sat on the same cushions as the day before.

'I need to explain to you how you can help us, don't I?' he said. We nodded and he went on, speaking slowly. 'How much do you know of the history of this period?'

'Nothing at all,' Augie admitted rather guiltily.

'Me neither,' I said, wishing I had paid more attention in history classes. We looked at him expectantly.

'Perhaps I should give you a quick history lesson then.' We waited and, after a pause, he said, 'Well, about a hundred and fifty years ago, after the Romans had finally left this land, the people were Pagans and divided into small tribes, all warring with each other. Slowly the Church asserted itself across the country and the tribes became more unified. Are you with me so far?' We were concentrating hard and, in spite of some of the difficult words, we did understand most of what he was saying so we nodded at him to continue.

'Good. Well, there were setbacks along the way, most notably when, about a hundred years ago, Penda, the Pagan king of Mercia, killed the newly Christian king of Northumbria in battle and the land reverted to Paganism for a while.' He shuddered at the memory as if he had actually been there himself which, for all we knew, he had. Then he went on,

'But Christianity came back, as it always does, and we are living now in fairly stable times. But there are big storm clouds on the horizon and things are looking more uncertain every day. Our present King, Ceolwulf, is a scholar like me but he is a weak king and the people are not willing to follow him. Also there are still plenty of people who say they are Christian but, in fact, still secretly worship the old Pagan gods. If these people unified under a different leader, they could do great harm to us here. And finally, there are reports of wild men coming from the East in long boats who are preparing to ravage this land. All this is why I am worried. Do you understand?'

'Yes, I think so,' Augie said. Then turning to me he added excitedly, 'The wild men from the East must be the Vikings!'

I was watching Father Bede, waiting for him to come to the point, and just nodded and said, 'Maybe.'

Father Bede then said, as if reading my mind, 'I know you are impatient to hear how you can help us. Well, now I can tell you. We have here in Jarrow two manuscripts which I want very much to preserve. The first is a great example of the art of our time and is a book of the Gospels, written in Lindisfarne in the North, a number of years ago. It was sent to us for safekeeping since Lindisfarne is even more exposed to danger than we are. The second is a book of my own which I have called the History of the English Church and People. I have just finished it after many years work and it is the first book of its kind. That is why the room is so cluttered,' he said, looking around at the piles of paper he was surrounded by. 'I believe that the two manuscripts will be valuable for future generations but, with all the present dangers we are surrounded by, I do not wish to keep them here. I would rather send them to a place of real safety where they can be properly protected.' Then he stopped and looked directly at us.

'Go on,' I said eagerly.

'I need somebody completely reliable to take them to the King in York who could look after them properly. It could be a perilous journey and I can't ask any of my people here to go. Nor can I go myself. The monastery needs me here. I think you two with your great horses which could outrun any danger would be the perfect messengers.'

We were speechless at his suggestion and then I burst out, 'But we are only children!'

'So you say. But I see the beginnings of greatness in you both and God has clearly sent you to me for this one task. Don't worry. You will be as well prepared for the journey as we can make you.' And with that compliment and reassurance he clearly felt that we could not disobey his orders. And orders they were, I was quite sure of that. Then suddenly changing the subject, he asked 'Do you have any talents?'

I replied, 'Well, I sing a bit and play the piano and Augie plays the recorder.'

'Music! I hadn't thought of that. Perfect! I don't know what a piano or a recorder is but I'm sure we can find you some instruments around here somewhere.' Perfect for what I wondered but decided to keep the question for another time. We had too much to think about as it was. Then he changed the subject yet again. 'Would you like to meet some other children?'

'Yes, please!' Augie said enthusiastically.

I remembered my thought over breakfast and wondered again whether Father Bede was a mind reader.

'I thought you might,' he said and called out, 'Wilbert, can you come in here?'

A boy appeared from what must have been the next room, a bit older than us with long dark hair and dressed in a simple tunic like ours. 'This is Wilbert, my scribe,' Father Bede said proudly. 'Wilbert, this is

August and June.' He bowed to us and we bowed back to him. 'I want you to show them around. Introduce them to other children. Oh, and see if you can find them some musical instruments.'

'Yes, master,' Wilbert replied. 'Come,' he said and we knew we were dismissed. So we left with the boy, wondering where he would take us.

Chapter 6

Wilbert led us out of the monastery and around to the back where we hadn't been before. There, a short distance away, we saw a proper village with people doing all sorts of interesting things outside their thatched huts. Some were making baskets, others skinning dead animals and yet others making pots. It looked like a thriving community and I shuddered to think what would become of it if the Vikings ever landed here. And there were children! Lots of them! Playing in the street if you could call the rough path between the huts a street. I wanted to stop and ask them what games they were playing but Wilbert was striding on ahead of us, right through the village and out the other side to where a single hut stood on its own. We still hadn't exchanged a single word with him.

He went straight up to it and through its open door into the interior. We followed him with some trepidation since we knew not what waited for us in the gloom.

Inside it was simply furnished with wooden chairs and table and a couple of straw beds in the corner. It appeared to have very little else in it, including people. There was nobody inside it at all. 'Sit', he commanded and we sat on two of the hard chairs around the table while he sat down opposite us. There was a fierce light of intelligence in his eyes.

'We'll take it in turns to ask questions,' he said. 'You start.'

'OK. A game.' Augie said. 'Whose house is this?'

'It was my family's. But I suppose it's mine now,' Wilbert responded sadly.

'Where are they?' I asked.

'All dead of the plague. After they died, Father Bede took me in and taught me everything I know.'

'The plague?' I gasped. Here was another horror of this age we hadn't bargained on. As if Vikings weren't bad enough!

'Yes, you know what that is, don't you?' he asked.

'Yes, of course we do but we don't have plague where we come from,' Augie said.

'Lucky you,' whispered Wilbert wistfully. And then I could see him for what he was, a bright boy who longed above all else to have his family back again. Then he pulled himself together and said, 'It's my turn now. Where are you from? I heard you were from some faraway country but which?'

'Eastport,' I said hurriedly to forestall the possibility of Augie giving away the truth. 'It's way to the South beyond the sea.' At least it wasn't a complete lie.

'Is it hot there?' asked Wilbert.

'A bit warmer than here,' I said. That seemed to satisfy him as he said, 'OK. Your turn now.'

'How did you become Father Bede's scribe?' Augie asked.

'I think it was because I was the only one who could decipher his writing,' Wilbert replied, grinning.

'Your turn again,' I said.

'I heard a little of your talk with Father Bede this morning and gathered that he wants to send you both on an important mission. Is that true?'

We wriggled uncomfortably and I finally said, 'Yes, something like that.'

'Would it be by any chance to take two manuscripts to York?'

'Did you happen to hear that as well?' Augie answered with a question of his own.

'No, I didn't but I know he's been waiting and praying for somebody strong enough to come and take them. And then you two turn up. A bit of a coincidence, wouldn't you say?'

'OK. It's true, yes,' I said, feeling instinctively we could trust this boy.

'Thank you for telling me the truth.' Then he continued, 'Can I come with you? I know the way and can protect you if you meet any trouble. I'm a good fighter.' This all came out in a rush and Augie and I both sat back and looked at each other incredulously.

'Why would you want to do that?' I asked.

'I want to do something important to repay Father Bede for all his kindness to me.'

'Fair enough,' Augie said, looking at me. 'Personally I'd love you to come with us if we are really going.'

'Me too,' I added.

'That's great!' and he let out a whoop of joy. Then he said softly, 'I hope Father Bede lets me go.'

'Oh, I think we can persuade him, don't you, Augie?' I said.

Augie nodded and said, 'Welcome to the expedition,' and the three of us stood up and hugged.

Then, after we had sat down again, Augie asked Wilbert, 'At the end of our conversation this morning, Father Bede mentioned something about us being properly prepared for the expedition. What did he mean, do you think?'

'Oh, I imagine with the right provision and weapons and stuff.'

'Weapons,' I gasped, 'What sort of weapons?'

'Whatever you are used to fighting with, I guess.'

'But neither of us is used to fighting and especially not with weapons!' I almost wailed.

'Really? And I suppose you came all the way from your country unarmed, did you?' Wilbert asked in disbelief.

'Yes, as a matter of fact, we did,' Augie said.

Wilbert looked at us wonderingly and then said, 'You must have some powerful magic to protect you.'

'Yes, I guess we must,' I said.

'Have you seen our horses?' Augie asked.

'No, I haven't,' Wilbert replied.

'Well, they are our magic,' Augie said and I suddenly realised that he was right.

'I'm looking forward to seeing them then. Now, I need to find you some musical instruments, don't I?'

'Yes, although we have no idea why we need them,' I said.

'It's probably some devious plan of his. Anyway, follow me.' And he led the way out of his house with a new bounce in his step and back into the village, straight to another hut. 'This is our music maker's house,' he said proudly.

Outside the house, sitting cross-legged in the street, was a man in his thirties probably who was whittling something out of a piece of wood.

'Good morning, Wilbert,' he said when we approached. 'Have you brought somebody to visit me?'

'Good morning, Egbert,' Wilbert said in return, adding, 'Father Bede would like you to show these two your instruments.'

Egbert looked us up and down and then said, 'Father Bede, eh? Well, you'd better come in then.'

So we went on into his house which was different to Wilbert's only in that it was cluttered with many instruments, both stringed and woodwind, most of which I didn't recognise.

'Do you two play then?' he asked us.

'I play the recorder and June plays the piano,' Augie said.

'Sorry. I have never heard of those instruments but you are welcome to look around and see if anything takes your fancy.'

So we did and at first couldn't find anything we could play but then Augie spotted something lying in a corner. It looked like a smooth cylinder of wood with a number of holes cut into the top but then I noticed that it had a thumb hole underneath and, although it didn't have a normal mouthpiece, I presumed it was some kind of early recorder. Augie picked it up and brought it back to Egbert.

'What is this?' he asked.

'Oh, it doesn't have a name. It's just something I made for my own amusement.'

'Can I try it?'

'By all means.'

In spite of its strangeness, Augie seemed to know instinctively what to do with it and put it to his lips and blew into one end. After a squeaky false start and some practice, he finally managed to make it sound something like his recorder back at home. 'Can I borrow it please?' he asked.

'No but you **can** have it. You can play it better than me.'

'Thanks a lot, Egbert,' Augie said.

As there was nothing in the house I could play, we left with Augie clutching his recorder.

'Good. That's one errand done,' Wilbert said. 'Do you still want to meet some children?'

'If you know any about our age, it would be nice,' I replied.

'How old are you then?' he asked.

'We are eleven. How old are you?'

'I'm fourteen. I'll introduce you both to a couple of my friends. One's a boy and one's a girl. They are twins and orphans like me. They are a couple of years older than you.'

'That would be nice,' I said. 'Thanks a lot.'

'They're out working in the fields at the moment but they will be back home soon for lunch.'

'Working? And they're only fourteen?' I said, aghast.

'Of course. We all have to work here from soon after we can walk. How old are children when they are put to work in your country?'

'Sixteen at the youngest,' Augie said and it was Wilbert's turn to look astonished.

'Amazing!' he said. Then he added, 'We'll have lunch here in the village. There's nobody waiting for you back at the monastery, is there?'

'No, I don't think so,' I said.

I caught Augie looking at me and knew what he was thinking. What else were we going to have to learn about this society, so similar in some ways to ours and yet so different in others? Oh well, I thought, at least human nature doesn't change and we seem to have fallen in with a group of very nice people.

Chapter 7

We crossed to the other side of the village where a small river was running through the countryside. There were a number of very young children splashing in the water but not an adult in sight. We sat on the bank watching them and looking out over the fields beyond. After a few minutes Augie began to get restless and whispered to Wilbert, 'I need to go to the toilet.' Wilbert looked at him uncomprehendingly at first but then understood and said, 'Oh, you mean the privy. Every house has one behind it. Choose any one you like.'

Augie got up and left, returning a few minutes later, looking rather pale. He sat down next to me and whispered, 'Another 'interesting' experience,' putting the word 'interesting' in quotation marks. 'I'm not surprised they have plague here.' But before he could elaborate, Wilbert stood up and waved at two children who were coming towards us. They ran up to him, shouting 'Wilbert!' excitedly. They were clearly twins, having very similar features and the same light brown hair. Their bodies were burnt a deep shade of brown from the sun.

Wilbert made the introductions, saying, pointing to the boy, 'Cuthbert, this is June and August. And,' pointing to the girl, 'this is Alkelda.'

'June and August,' murmured Alkelda. 'What strange names.'

'They have travelled far to help us,' Wilbert explained.

'Good to meet you both,' the boy, Cuthbert, said. Then to Wilbert, 'Where have you been? We haven't seen you for ages!'

'Yes, I know. Sorry about that but Father Bede's been keeping me very busy.'

'Oh well, you're here now. That's what matters,' the girl, Alkelda said. 'Come on back and have some lunch with us.'

'I was hoping you were going to say that,' Wilbert said, grinning.

So we all trooped back to their hut where Alkelda quickly put out plates and knives for all of us and then wooden beakers. She brought a jug of water from a cupboard and filled our beakers. Then she got out a big loaf of bread and a large hunk of cheese and said graciously to Augie and me, 'Please help yourselves.'

'Thank you,' we said together and we were all soon tucking in. The cheese and bread were lovely and I wondered why we could not make such tasty food in the 21st century. When we had all finished, Alkelda cleared everything away and then sat down again at the table.

She said, 'It's nice to meet new friends of Wilbert's.'

'It's nice to meet you two as well,' I said. 'And thanks for a lovely meal. Did you make the bread yourself?'

'I'm glad you enjoyed it. Yes, of course I did and the cheese as well.'

'You are clever!' I said admiringly. Then I asked one of the questions I had had in mind for a while. 'Can you tell us what kinds of games you like playing?'

'Oh, we're too old now for childish games,' her brother said. 'And too busy. But we do like play fighting, don't we, Alkelda?'

She nodded and he went over to a dark corner of the small room and came back carrying two wooden swords, a couple of small shields and two stout sticks.

'Would you like to show us your fighting skills,' Cuthbert said.

'I'm afraid we don't have any such skills,' I admitted shamefacedly.

But then Augie said, 'But I'm willing to learn. Can you show me?' And Cuthbert passed him a sword and shield and they were soon fighting away outside on the grass with Wilbert cheering them on.

Alkelda and I sat and watched them until Alkelda turned to me and said, 'Would you like to see my treasures?' I said I would like that very much and she led me back inside. She went over to one of the beds and pulled from under it a small wooden box. She opened it and I looked inside. There was a beautiful gold bracelet, a small doll and a couple of big sea shells. She explained to me that the bracelet had been her mother's who had given it to her just before she died while the doll had been hers when she was little. She had found the sea shells on the beach when she had once been to the seaside.

I could see her fighting to hold back the tears when she told me about her mother and I put my arms around her and hugged her. This seemed to comfort her and she dried her eyes with the back of her hand. She put her treasures away and then said out of the blue, 'I like you, June.'

'I like you too, Alkelda,' I said truthfully, wondering what it would be like to grow up without parents to love you and hug you. 'Did your parents die of the plague like Wilbert's?' I asked her gently.

'Yes, at much the same time. It was terrible.'

I thought she was going to start crying again so I quickly changed the subject. 'What do you do in the fields when you're working?' I asked, honestly curious to know the answer.

'We do everything the adults do,' she replied. 'It depends on the season. Now it's summer so we have to help bring the grain harvest in. In spring we plant the new crops and in winter we prepare food to keep, like the cheese you had for lunch.'

'It must be very hard for you,' I said.

'Oh, it's not too bad once you get used to it.'

'Can you read?'

'Oh, no!' She laughed now. 'I'm not a scholar like Wilbert.'

'Can any of the people in the village read and write?' I asked.

'No. Reading and writing are the preserve of the monks and their scribes. Anyway, what do we need with reading and writing?'

That shut me up and I couldn't think of any more questions for her. I felt I was at last starting to understand this society where everything was so much simpler than in the 21st century. It was a hard struggle to survive here and I remembered reading that in the old days most children died when they were very young and most adults didn't live much past forty. On the other hand, the very simplicity of their lives meant that they weren't all stressed out like adults, and many children too, in my own time. In fact, they may well have been happier. This last thought was a revelation but I put it to one side for consideration when I had more evidence.

We went back outside to find that Wilbert had taken over from Augie who was sitting on the ground nursing a bruise on the side of his face. 'It's more difficult than it looks,' he said, watching the two boys parry with their wooden swords. Then with a mighty blow Wilbert knocked Cuthbert's sword right out of his hand and raised his own in triumph. 'I win!' he cried.

'Yes, but you're a year older than me,' Cuthbert shot back at him.

'Anyway, it's good to see you two again,' Wilbert said. 'I think you need to get back to work, don't you?'

Cuthbert looked at the sun and said regretfully, 'Yes, it's time.'

'We must get back too. Otherwise Father Bede will start wondering what's happened to us.'

So we said our goodbyes and I gave Alkelda another hug. Then we were on our way back to the monastery.

Chapter 8

As we were approaching the main door of the monastery, Wilbert suddenly said, 'I've just remembered about your horses. Can I see them before we go in?' So we led him round to the stables and went in. We saw them at once in their stalls, their coats looking lustrous in the rays of light slanting through the wooden door from the late afternoon sunshine. They stood tall and proud, their long muscular legs and necks shown off to perfection. They looked at us and then bent their heads to let us pat them. Wilbert was astonished. 'Never have I seen such magnificent animals. I can understand what you meant now when you said they were your magic.' We made a fuss of the horses and they seemed to enjoy the attention.

Then, regretfully, it was time to go and we said goodbye to them with a promise that we would be back soon to ride them. They pricked up their ears when they heard this and whinnied softly. 'They seem to understand you,' Wilbert said amazed.

'Of course they do,' Augie said and we left it at that.

Upon our return to the monastery, we went straight to Father Bede's study and Wilbert knocked. He called us in and we stood in a row in front of his desk. Father Bede immediately noticed the bruise on Augie's face and said, 'Have you been fighting, young August?'

Yes, master, but it was only play fighting and I really enjoyed it.'

Wilbert cut in here, saying, 'I introduced them to my friends, Cuthbert and Alkelda. We had lunch with them.'

'I know those two. Nice children, if a bit wild.' Then Father Bede said, 'And what's that you're holding, August?' Augie showed it to him and he looked at it with interest. 'A musical instrument, eh? Can you play it?'

'Not very well yet,' Augie admitted.

'Play me something,' Father Bede commanded and Augie raised the recorder to his lips and played a couple of scales. Then he launched into one of his Grade 4 pieces which he had played for me often in our previous lives. Considering that he had only had it for such a short time, I thought he did pretty well.

When he had finished, we all clapped and he blushed modestly. 'Thank you,' he said.

'It will do well, August,' Father Bede said. 'Now can you play something which June can sing along to?' That took us both aback and we looked at each other.

'I . . . . I don't think so,' Augie said hesitantly.

'Well, I want you two to go away and practise until you can,' Father Bede said decisively.

'Yes, Father,' we chorused obediently.

'Now, what else do you want to say to me? I can see from Wilbert's expression that he has something.'

Now it was Wilbert's turn to blush and he said after a short pause, 'I would like to go with them on their mission.'

'Oh, so you know about that, do you?' Father Bede murmured pensively.

'Yes, I do. There are many good reasons for me to go and August and June have said they are willing to have me along,' Wilbert stated almost defiantly.

I spoke for the first time. 'Not just willing,' I said. 'We really want him to come with us.'

'Let me think about it,' Father Bede said. 'Anything else?'

'Yes,' I said. 'I would very much like to see these Gospels that you said we have to take.' I had been thinking about them while we were walking back from the village.

'I will show them to you now,' Father Bede said. And getting up from his chair, he went across to a small cupboard set in the wall which I hadn't noticed before, taking a key out from inside his robes. He unlocked the door of the cupboard and brought out a large leather-bound volume with its cover decorated with many jewels. When he opened it, we both gasped with astonishment. It was filled with not only writing but some of the most beautiful pictures we had ever seen. There were many scenes which I recognised from my Bible studies class and the paintings were so realistic and the colours so vibrant that they seemed to leap right out of the pages at us.

'Wow!' I said. 'That is incredible!'

'Perhaps you can understand now why I want to keep it safe. Many a Pagan would like to get his hands on it and burn it,' Father Bede said.

'Yes, I understand now,' I said and Augie added, 'Me too.'

Then Father Bede said, 'If you two can prepare a couple of songs for me, I think you will be ready to leave tomorrow. Wilbert, I need you here to help me pack up the Gospels and my own manuscript.'

'Yes, master,' he said.

Then he said to us, 'I'll see you again after supper.'

We knew we were dismissed and went out and back to our own small room where we discussed for a while some tunes which were easy to play and which I knew the words of. We finally decided on Old McDonald and Ten Green Bottles which we practised for a while until I could sing along with the recorder. 'I hope he'll be happy with those,' Augie muttered and I said, 'Yes, well, he'll have to be, won't he?' Then Augie played me some more of his Grade 4 pieces, more confidently this time.

We talked for a bit about the day and then Sister Ethelreda appeared and called us to supper. So we went with her back to the kitchen where we had another delicious bowl of hot stew and more of their scrumptious bread. Then, full and a bit sleepy, we went back again to Father Bede's study where we were welcomed in. He asked us to play and sing for him which we did with him tapping along with the rhythm on his desktop. When we had finished, he said, 'That will do very nicely, children. Now let me explain why I wanted you to do that.' He paused but then continued, 'I want you to go in the guise of travelling musicians. They are not usually bothered by people, even bad ones. Everybody likes a good tune. The only problem I can see is your horses which any bandit would covet but I think they can look after themselves.' He stopped but then added, 'Oh, and I am sure the King in York will enjoy hearing you play too.'

'OK,' Augie said. 'Have you decided whether Wilbert can come with us yet?'

'Yes. He convinced me it was a good idea. He can go as your servant.'

'Oh, great!' I said. 'Thank you very much.'

'That's OK,' he said. 'Now run along and get some rest. It will be a busy day for you two tomorrow. My people are preparing everything you will need.'

'Goodnight, Father,' we said and left. We went back to our own room and lay down but were too excited to sleep for a bit. We talked about our new upcoming adventure and just before we went to sleep, Augie said to me, 'Have you noticed how quiet it is here at night compared to at home? There is no traffic sound at all.' I listened and realised he was right and then fell fast asleep and slept almost dreamlessly until the following morning.

Chapter 9

The next morning Sister Ethelreda bustled in at sunrise and said, 'It's nearly time for breakfast. Are you two ready? I hear you are leaving us today.' We nodded sleepily and began to get washed and in a few minutes were ready to follow her back to the kitchen. There we had breakfast and then she took us back again to Father Bede's study. We sat on the cushions and looked at him. He was writing something on a piece of parchment but he soon finished and, when he had, he folded the paper and sealed it with some wax and a big stamp he had sitting on his desk. Then he passed it to me saying, 'June, this is a letter from me to King Alcuin in York, telling him who you are and explaining your mission. Keep it safe.'

'Yes, Father,' I said and I put it inside my tunic top next to my skin.

'Go now and collect your other clothes. You may not be returning here and you will need them if you go back to your own time. I will meet you at the stables.'

'Yes, Father,' we chorused obediently. And we left.

'Why did Father Bede give the letter to you, not me?' Augie asked jealously.

'I've no idea but, if you want it, you can have it,' I said. That surprised him but it also shut him up and I was to hear no more from him on the subject of the letter.

We picked up our modern clothes from our room and then walked over to the stables. I was feeling more afraid every second and, looking at Augie, I knew he felt the same. Neither of us wanted to be wrenched from the safety of the monastery and sent out into the wide, and obviously wicked, world.

When we got to the stables, Wilbert was already there, saddling up the old mare of Father Bede's. He saw us and beamed with delight. 'So we're really off,' he said.

'It looks that way,' I said, trying to squash the feeling of fear in the pit of my stomach.

'Why are you taking your master's horse?' Augie asked and Wilbert replied, 'The good Father suggested it himself. He said the horses knew and could protect each other. Northelm is a clever old horse.'

Augie accepted this explanation and we went over to where Pegasus and Black Beauty were waiting patiently outside their stalls. They had already been saddled and looked resplendent in their bridles and harnesses. Each of them had two large leather saddlebags attached to their backs and hanging over their flanks. After giving each horse a good pat, we opened the bags to see what was inside. Black Beauty's held two large heavy parcels, carefully wrapped in cloth, obviously the two manuscripts, while Pegasus's had what looked like a lot of provisions in them. There was just room for our modern clothes.

At that moment Cuthbert and Alkelda came running in. Cuthbert said breathlessly, 'We heard you were leaving. I wanted to give to something to keep you safe on your journey, Wilbert.' And he handed him a wicked-looking dagger with an engraved handle. 'It was my father's and I thought it might be useful. I know that Father Bede would never give you such a thing. He disapproves of violence but, if the worst comes to the worst, I reckon you need something to defend yourself and June and August with.'

'Thank you very much, Cuthbert. I hope I won't need it but it was most thoughtful of you,' Wilbert said. 'I will bring it back safe and sound.' And he put the dagger away inside his own bag which he had slung over his shoulder.

Then we all gave each other a final hug and Alkelda whispered in my ear, 'You are wiser than the two boys. Look after them.' I was surprised at her words but nodded and she smiled at me. Then the twins ran out almost bumping into Father Bede as he came striding in with Sister Ethelreda bustling close behind him.

She came up to Augie and me, also giving us a big hug each. There were tears in her eyes and in mine too. Then she turned to Wilbert saying sternly, "You do your duty, young man, and don't get up to any mischief!'

'No, Sister,' Wilbert replied meekly.

'That's enough of that,' Father Bede said with a twinkle in his eye. 'Are you ready?'

'I think so, master,' Wilbert said.

'Good. Then let's not waste any more time.' And he helped first me up into Pegasus's saddle and then Augie onto Black Beauty. Wilbert jumped easily onto Northelm and then we were off and away from the relative security of the monastery, our great horses moving slowly to keep pace with Northelm.

Chapter 10

$\mathbf{S}$oon we had left the monastery far behind and were trotting along the ruins of what Wilbert explained to us was once a great Roman road. He added that this road should take us straight to York which he had visited once with Father Bede. It was open country and there were fields on either side of us with a few people working in them. We felt safe enough here but we stayed vigilant and didn't talk much. After a couple of hours' riding, Wilbert suggested we stopped for lunch. We left the horses to graze at the side of the road and sat on the grass eating some of the food in my saddlebags.

Then we continued on our way and I guess we became over-confident. We were now chatting together and had moved into a forest where the trees were close together and the roadway barely visible. Suddenly Northelm pricked up her ears and stopped. We stopped too and listened hard for any kind of danger. Then we heard it. The clip-clopping of many hooves moving in our direction.

We immediately left the road and hid in the forest where we could watch but not be seen—we hoped. The horses we had heard came into view and we saw a number of men, armed to the teeth with swords, spears and battleaxes, but who were clearly not regular soldiers as they were not wearing any kind of uniform. 'Brigands!' whispered Wilbert. 'Keep very quiet!' Our horses seemed to understand the idea and stood stock still while we scarcely breathed. I thought I was going to sneeze and had to pinch my nose hard to stop any sound escaping.

The brigands seemed to be led by a huge man who appeared to be dressed in a bearskin and was even more festooned with weapons than his comrades. He had a bushy dark beard and was wearing a helmet with horns on it. He looked fearsome.

Fortunately none of them detected us as they filed past talking amongst themselves and, after they had passed, we breathed a huge collective sigh of relief. Wilbert, however, told us to stay where we were for a bit longer. When the forest was completely silent again, Wilbert said to us in a worried tone of voice, 'I don't know where they were from. I didn't understand their language. Could they be the dreaded Norsemen?'

I shot a warning look at Augie who, like me, had understood the language perfectly. Our translation devices in our brains seemed to enable us to make sense of any language around us. We knew that they were indeed a raiding party of Vikings who were looking for loot and women. But I just said, 'I suppose it's possible but there's nothing we can do about them. We have to press on.'

'Yes, but where were they going?' Wilbert asked.

'No idea,' Augie said. We both knew he was worried about his village and the monastery but we also knew that our priority was to get the two manuscripts to a safe place. I felt sorry for anyone who got caught by those savage-looking men but there was nothing we could do for them.

So we left our hiding place and went back onto the road again, this time being doubly vigilant. We continued on through the forest for some time and finally broke out into open countryside again where we felt safer. We started talking about our lucky escape but Wilbert pointed to some hills ahead of us and said, 'If there is to be real danger that is where we'll find it. We have to cross those hills before we get on the plain leading to York.'

'Is there no other way?' I asked anxiously.

'I'm afraid not,' Wilbert replied.

So we carried on in silence, each of us preoccupied with our own thoughts. As we got closer to the hills, I could see the landscape more clearly. In any other circumstances I would have called it beautiful with its areas of forest and waterfalls outlined against the clear blue sky.

'Are we going to be able to cross before night falls?' Augie asked.

Wilbert looked at the sun and said, 'I think not. We need to find somewhere to camp.' I didn't know about Augie but I had never been camping in my life. It sounded like fun.

There were no houses or people to be seen here, just a few burnt-out ruins, and the ground itself was hard and stony with very little grass, which we knew was essential for the horses. We just had to keep going. Then, as we started to approach the uplands, we came to a dip in the land and below us we could see a small river running through an empty valley. Water and grass! The two things we needed. The sky was getting perceptibly darker now and we hurried down to the river bank. The water was pure and sweet and the three of us slaked our thirst after our long ride in the hot sun while the horses did the same.

'We need to make a fire,' Wilbert said. 'It gets cold outside at night.'

'How are we going to do that?' Augie asked curiously.

'Easy enough. If the two of you could find me some wood, I'll get it going in no time. I'll unpack some essentials.'

We bowed to his superior knowledge of these things and went off to look for firewood. We didn't have to go far as there were a few trees nearby which had plenty of wood buried under the dry leaves. We took as much as we could carry and went back to Wilbert. When he had arranged the wood to his satisfaction, he took what he told us were two pieces of flint out of his bag. Then he struck them against each other and hey presto there was a spark. It didn't work first time. It took several goes but he soon had the fire burning merrily. We watched all this with fascination as we had only read about such things in some of our adventure stories.

He had already prepared the food and we sat in the gathering twilight eating and chatting. I had been right. It was a lot of fun. After supper we took the blankets we had brought from the saddlebags and laid them on the grass. The boys were asleep as soon as it became properly dark but I stayed awake looking up at the stars which were incredibly clear in the night sky. I knew that they wouldn't change a bit over the next 1200 years and that knowledge made me feel very insignificant.

I finally dozed off but was awoken by something, I didn't know what, in the middle of the night. I looked around. The boys were sleeping soundly but the horses seemed restless. They were moving their heads in an agitated way from side to side and this was making their harnesses jingle. That must have been what woke me up. I punched Augie lightly and whispered, 'Wake up!' He opened his eyes and looked at me. 'The horses are restless,' I said quietly. 'Something's wrong!' He looked at them and said, 'It's late. Go back to sleep.' And with those words he turned over and was soon snoring lightly again. But I was sure something wasn't right.

I got up wanting to put some more wood on the fire so I could see better. We had some left over from the previous night and the embers were still glowing. I threw the remains of the wood on the fire and they hissed and crackled till they caught alight and sent a pillar of flame up into the night sky. I looked carefully around and suddenly I saw them! We seemed to be completely surrounded by a pack of lean, hungry-looking wolves! They had shrunk back into the shadows when I had put the new wood on the fire but now, fearless, they were coming closer. I screamed for the boys to wake up which they did at once. Wilbert saw immediately what was happening and took his knife out of his belt where he was keeping it now. 'Keep back,' he commanded and Augie and I stood close behind him, completely terrified, and waited for the wolves to attack.

The leader of the pack, or the one I assumed was the leader, a monstrous grey beast, came right out of the darkness now and must have recognised us as mere children because, totally unafraid, he prowled up to the saddlebags with the food and started rooting around in them. The others followed him and it was now that I made my mistake. I shouted at them to go away. The leader turned to me, his eyes glowing red in the firelight, and suddenly pounced right onto Wilbert who was standing there bravely waving his knife. He was knocked to the ground by the wolf's weight and the knife fell out of his hand. Then Augie, even more bravely, picked it up and thrust it hard into the wolf's back which was turned to him. The wolf howled in agony and fell off Wilbert onto its back. But he at once jumped up, apparently unhurt, and pulling the knife out of the wolf, plunged it into its heart. The wolf stopped its writhing and lay still. The others had seen the fight and slunk off quickly into the darkness.

We were all shaking with fear, me most of all, but Wilbert commanded us to load up the horses as quickly as we could. We had to get out of that place before the wolves decided to come back. We managed to save some of the food which had not been eaten by those awful creatures and put it back in the saddlebags. Then we put the blankets and the few other things we had used away and went over to the horses which were still restless. They could still smell the wolves. I asked Pegasus to kneel so I could put the bags of the remaining food onto her back and Augie did the same with Black Beauty. I checked that the precious books were OK and then we all scrambled back onto our horses and were soon cantering away from that blood-soaked place, leaving the carcass of the wolf on the ground for the crows. Although it was still pitch dark, the horses had no problem finding the way and we were soon back on the road again, heading for York.

Chapter 11

We cantered along for a way with Northelm trying valiantly to keep up when we heard Wilbert shout at us to stop. We waited for him to catch up and, when he had, he said, 'I think I'm hurt.' We slid off our horses and he managed to get off his old mare. We could just see his face in the starlight and he was obviously in pain. I could see his right arm and it was black with dark blood oozing from a great scratch on it. I said to Augie, 'This looks serious. The wolf must have scratched him when it attacked.'

'What can we do?' he asked.

'The first thing is to bandage the wound so that it stops bleeding,' I said.

'What with?' he asked.

'Can you find me a piece of clean cloth?' I said. 'Unfortunately, we have no water with us to wash it.'

He looked down at the sleeve of his tunic and then asked Wilbert for his knife. He grimaced with pain but managed to pull it from his belt. Augie then wiped the blade on some grass and sliced off a sleeve of his tunic, passing it to me. I wound it tightly round Wilbert's arm and tied it as tightly as I could.

'That's the best we can do for the moment. We need to get you to a doctor, Wilbert,' I said.

'There are no doctors between here and York,' he replied. We all looked at each other and wondered what to do.

'You might bleed to death if we don't get you there quickly,' I said.

'But how can we do that?' Augie said. 'Northelm could never keep us with us.'

Then Wilbert spoke. 'I have an idea,' he said. 'If I could ride with you on one of your horses, I'm sure Northelm could find her own way to York.'

'Really?' I said.

'Yes,' he said simply.

'OK. That's what we'll do then,' I said.

Wilbert went over to Northelm and told her to follow us to York. She seemed to understand and I swear she nodded her head. Then, with Black Beauty kneeling on the ground, Augie helped Wilbert up onto its back and he sat behind Augie holding tightly round his waist. I mounted myself and told the horses to go fast but gently and, with a last look back at Northelm, we sped off. The horses appeared to understand the urgency for we galloped, our horses' hooves hardly seeming to touch the ground, through the hills and down onto the plain beyond. Nobody could have stopped us. We were much too fast.

Tireless, the horses sped on through the night with me keeping a careful eye on Wilbert in case he fell off Black Beauty. And, as dawn finally broke, we could see in the distance a large town. I galloped up to Augie's side and shouted at Wilbert through the rushing wind, 'Is that York?' He looked ahead, squinting through tears of pain, and shouted back, 'Yes.'

Good, I thought. Not long now. And, indeed, we soon came to civilisation, people working in the fields and huts dotting the landscape. Day was fully upon us now and we dashed through several villages, the people looking up startled as we sped by. Then we finally came to the city itself surrounded by huge stone walls. There was a gate open with people travelling in and out and we went through, just trotting now, Augie letting me go first.

'A message for the King!' I shouted in my loudest voice. People stopped and stared. I realised that they weren't looking at us but at our magnificent horses which were sweating freely now after their long gallop. They let us pass, obviously thinking that we must be important to have such horses and we were escorted by a soldier up to the most imposing building in the city, clearly the King's palace. Wilbert was as white as a sheet now, probably from blood loss, and I knew our first priority was to get him to a doctor who could properly treat his wound.

We went into a courtyard inside the building and there we slipped off our horses and I marched ahead, looking as confident as I could, with Augie behind me, half dragging, half carrying Wilbert. A well-dressed courtier, if that's what he was, came up to us and asked us what we wanted. I told him to take us directly to the King who would be very unhappy if he didn't. He seemed cowed by my certainty and led us into the palace to a large inner chamber.

In the room there was a big throne with an imposing-looking man sitting on it, with a dark beard and gorgeous robes. This must be the king, I thought excitedly. He was listening to a man who seemed to have some sort of grievance but I paid no attention to him and going directly up to the King, said, 'We have come directly from Father Bede in Jarrow with something important for you, Your Majesty.' I have no idea what he thought of us, three bedraggled children, one wounded, one missing a sleeve and myself unwashed with my hair all over the place. I took out the letter from Father Bede from inside my tunic and passed it to him. He read it quickly then looked at us in astonishment. Before he could say anything, however, I said, 'As you can see, our friend needs medical attention. Can you help him please, Sire?' And the King at once called for his own personal physician who arrived quickly and was ordered to give Wilbert the best attention possible. Finally, to my relief, he was taken away to be treated. Our biggest problem solved, I hoped.

Then the King said to me, 'Why did Father Bede have to send children to me?'

'We have the best horses, Sire,' I said simply and the courtier who had escorted us in whispered something in the King's ear.

Then he said, 'I must see these horses for myself.' And he led the way back to the courtyard where Pegasus and Black Beauty were waiting patiently. The King, whose name I remembered now was Alcuin, turned to us upon seeing them and said, 'You didn't exaggerate, did you? I would dearly love to have them for myself.' Then he remembered the letter and said, 'Where are these manuscripts you brought me?'

Augie went up to Black Beauty, undid his saddlebags and, pointing, said, 'In there.' The King then ordered a couple of his men who had followed him out to take them into his palace and look after them carefully. He would look at them later. Then he ordered the horses to be stabled and well cared for. When this was done, he said to us, 'Follow me.' And he led us back into the palace to a small comfortable room with no one in it. There he sat behind a beautifully inlaid desk and bade us sit on two chairs standing in front.

'Tell me the story of how you got here from Jarrow,' he said. So, with me doing most of the talking but Augie chipping in occasionally, we told him of our ride from Jarrow, how we had nearly been captured by Norsemen and how we had been surrounded by a pack of wolves but had managed to escape. That was how Wilbert had got injured, I explained. He listened quietly, not interrupting, and said, when I finally stumbled to a halt, 'You have done bravely, children, in fulfilling your task for Father Bede. But what you say about the Norsemen worries me. I had heard that a few advance parties had already landed in the country but I had no idea they were so close

to my own kingdom. Well, they are my problem now.'
And he looked serious for a while, not speaking. Then
he said, 'I must get a look-out posted for the other
horse you call Northelm.'

'Thank you, Your Majesty,' I said. 'It is Father Bede's
own horse and we know he would hate anything to
happen to it.'

'Is there anything else you want me to do?' he
asked.

'Can we see our friend?' Augie asked.

'Of course,' he replied. And he went outside and
called for one of the Queen's own ladies-in-waiting.
When she appeared, he put us in her charge telling
her to take us to Wilbert. Then he added, 'Give them
a bath and something to eat. Oh and find them some
new clothes and let them rest a while.' His final words
to us were, 'When you are rested, we'll talk some
more.'

Chapter 12

When we arrived in Wilbert's room, we were surprised to find it sumptuously furnished with him sitting up in bed being served hot broth by a pretty, young woman. His arm had been newly bandaged and his face had got a little of its old colour back. He beamed at us when we came in saying, 'This is the life, eh, you guys?'

Augie ran up to him and gave him an impulsive hug which made him wince in pain and he said, 'Careful, August, I'm still not well, you know.'

Augie apologised but then said, 'It's great to see you looking better anyway, Wilbert.'

He replied, 'The doctor says I will need a few days rest and then I'll be as right as rain although I'll have a big, honourable scar to remind me of our adventure.' Then he turned to me and asked, 'What news, June?'

'Well, the first and most important thing is that the King now has the manuscripts,' I said. 'And, nearly as important, he has posted a look-out for Northelm.'

'Good. But Northelm will get here safely, I'm sure.'

'What will you two do now?' he asked. 'Go back to your own country?'

'I'm not sure,' I said. 'It depends on Pegasus and Black Beauty.'

He looked puzzled at my words but then clearly decided to just accept them, knowing how important our horses were to us.

'OK,' he said. 'But you could just stay here and live in the lap of luxury, couldn't you?'

I laughed and said, 'No, I don't think we could do that although it's a tempting thought. Don't forget . . . .' and then I stopped because I had been going to say, 'we have people at home waiting for us' but I didn't want to remind him that we had families and he didn't.

But he caught on at once and said, 'I know what you were going to say, June, and I wouldn't have been offended if you had said it.'

'Thank you, Wilbert,' I said relieved.

Meanwhile the young woman who was serving Wilbert his broth was shuffling her feet restlessly and she suddenly said, 'The doctor has ordered Wilbert to rest. Can you two come back later?'

'Of course. We're sorry, Wilbert. We didn't want to tire you out,' Augie said. 'We'll see you later.'

We waved goodbye and left, accompanied by our own lady-in-waiting whose name we soon discovered was Edburga. She took us to a different part of the palace and into another beautifully furnished room. There she said, 'This is yours now while you stay here. Now, what would you like first, a bath, a meal or a rest?'

We both agreed that, after all that riding, a bath would be nice before we ate. Edburga nodded her approval and called in some servants who looked at our grubby clothes with distaste and asked them to prepare a bath for us. We were no longer embarrassed at having to undress in front of one another and we gave them our old clothes before padding naked next door where a big bath was being filled for us from large steaming jugs of water. We hopped in together after it was full and luxuriated in the hot water. We were even given some rough soap to wash ourselves with, the first we had seen in this age. We stayed in the bath for quite a while and it was only when the water started to cool that we finally got out. Edburga gave us big towels to dry ourselves on and we felt scrubbed clean.

Waiting for us in our bedroom were some truly gorgeous clothes, a long green silk dress for me with a kind of petticoat to go underneath and a purple satin tunic with an undershirt for Augie. We tried them on and they fitted perfectly. Edburga brought me a piece of finely burnished bronze which acted as a mirror and I admired myself in it. I had never before felt like such a fine young lady. Then Augie used it and simply said, 'Wow!'

Augie now asked Edburga if we could eat. He was hungry as usual. She said, laughing, 'I thought you might be. I have nephews and nieces about your age and they're always hungry. Wait here.' So we waited and she soon returned followed by two more servants bearing large silver plates on which were huge pieces of pork still sizzling gently and mounds of vegetables. We sat at the table in our room and devoured everything with Edburga looking on indulgently. When we had finished, Augie gave a discreet burp and said, 'That was absolutely scrumptious.' I agreed with him.

Then I realised that with all that food inside me I was feeling decidedly sleepy and yawned. After all, we had been riding most of the previous night. My yawn was infectious and Augie followed suit. Edburga said, 'It's time for you two to have a decent nap. I will come back later.' And she called the servants who had been waiting outside to clear the dishes away. Then she left after closing the shutters on the windows so it was dark in the room. There was only the one bed but it was enormous and we took off our outer layer of clothes, leaving only our undergarments on, and jumped in. It had looked comfortable and indeed it was. We covered ourselves with warm blankets and were soon asleep.

I had no idea what time it was when I woke up but Augie was still sleeping. I got out of bed, opened one of the shutters a bit, and saw it was still daylight outside. I sat on the bed and combed my hair, now dry after our bath, with a comb made of some sort of animal bone which had been left on the table. Then I slipped into my long green dress. Augie opened one eye and said, 'Why, June, you look as pretty as a picture.'

I blushed at the compliment and said, 'Don't be silly. Now get dressed and let's go exploring.'

'OK,' he said and jumped out of bed. He put his satin tunic on and said, 'It feels good to be wearing decent clothes again, doesn't it?'

I agreed and then had a thought. 'We need to check that our modern clothes are OK. We might need them soon.'

'Good thinking,' he said. 'They should still be in the saddlebags.'

'Yes, but where are **they**?' I asked.

'No idea. But we need to find out,' he said. And with that we ran out of our room.

Chapter 13

$\mathfrak{A}$s we left, I said to Augie, 'We should check the stables first. That's where we last saw the saddlebags.' He agreed and we left the palace, going round to the back where the stables were situated. When we got there, we went in and saw Pegasus and Black Beauty placidly eating hay, their coats gleaming and no trace of the sweat that had been on them earlier. There was a groom tending to them and we went up to him and I asked, 'Have you seen the saddlebags that were on these horses?'

'These be yours then?' the groom enquired in a strong, rural accent. He was amazed, seeing that we were only children.

'Yes, indeed,' I said.

'They be the best horses I have ever seen,' he said.

"Thank you,' I said. 'Now can you please answer my question?'

'Yes, young masters. They be over there,' he said, pointing to a dusty corner of the stables.

We went over and saw the saddlebags lying on the ground. We opened them and saw to our relief that nothing had been touched. We took out the remains of the dried food we had brought from the monastery and offered it to the groom who accepted it gratefully as payment for his services. Then we rescued our modern clothes and Augie's recorder and put them in an old cloth sack lying in the same corner.

We checked that the saddlebags were now empty and, giving the horses a friendly pat, we were about to leave when a soldier came in leading Northelm. We were so pleased to see her we made an enormous fuss of her and she whinnied in what we hoped was pleasure. Then she went over to our two great steeds and nuzzled them affectionately. We thanked the soldier and told the groom that she had been on a long journey and needed food and rest. He just nodded and we thanked him too. We knew Wilbert would be delighted with this piece of news.

Then we left but, before going to see him, we went back to our room and hid our modern clothes in a disused cupboard along with Augie's recorder.

After doing that, we made our way to Wilbert's room, looking in open doors as we passed them. We saw Edburga sewing a great tapestry but decided not to disturb her. Going on, we came finally to the door of Wilbert's room and were pleased to find it empty except for Wilbert himself who was sitting up in bed. We went in and he took a look at us and burst out laughing.

'What's so funny?' I asked crossly.

'Nothing. It's just that I never imagined you two as nobility. It was a shock,' he said.

'We have some news for you,' Augie then said. 'Northelm's back safe and sound and is in the stables with Pegasus and Black Beauty.'

'That **is** good,' he said. 'I told you she'd return safely, didn't I?'

'Yes, you did,' I said. Then I asked, 'Are you bored?'

'Not yet, thanks. I'm still getting my strength back,' he replied.

At that moment his nurse came in and shooed us out so we left without arguing.

We went back through the palace until we came to the room where Edburga was still sewing. This time we went in. She looked up and said, 'Now you look more presentable. June, I would like to do something with your hair before dinner.'

'When's that?' Augie asked eagerly, thinking about food as usual.

She smiled and said, 'Soon now. I'll just finish what I'm doing here.' And she carried on sewing. I watched her curiously, never having seen anybody actually in the process of producing anything so beautiful. It was a picture of a hunting scene, with stags and horses and their riders seeming to jump right out of the tapestry at you.

Wistfully, I said, 'I wish I could do that.'

'You mean you can't?' Edburga said astonished. 'What **do** they teach you in that country of yours?'

'Reading, writing and mathematics mainly,' I replied without thinking.

'Really?' she said in great puzzlement now. 'How extraordinary!' Fortunately she left it there and didn't ask any more questions but then she said, 'I could teach you if you want.'

'Could you really?' I cried in excitement.

'Yes, of course. But it takes a long time to learn to do it well.'

'That would be fantastic!' I said.

Augie meanwhile was standing there looking bored.

'Right. Finished,' Edburga said, snipping off a final piece of thread with her teeth and tying a tiny knot.

The three of us trooped back again to our room where she made Augie comb his red hair into something approaching order while she made two long plaits of mine before coiling them up and pinning them on either side of my head. I looked in the mirror and told her, 'I've never had my hair done like this before.'

'All young ladies have their hair done like that here,' she said.

Then Augie piped up. 'Are there any other children here in the palace?' he asked.

'Yes, sure,' she replied. 'There are the King's children. You will meet them at dinner. All except the baby, that is.'

'How old are they?' he asked again.

'Let me see,' she answered slowly. 'Alcuin the Younger is fifteen, Frisuthwith is twelve, Wicthed is ten and Cuthbert is six.'

'Oh, good,' he said. 'Maybe we can play with them later?'

'If the King gives his permission, I'm sure you can. Now come on. It's time for dinner.'

We followed her until we came to a great dining hall which was full of adults all chatting and laughing. I realised that I hadn't heard much real laughter since I arrived in this time. There were long tables with benches around them all covered with silver and gold crockery and cutlery and, upstairs in what I thought was called a minstrels' gallery, was a small group of musicians waiting patiently with their instruments on their laps. The floor was strewn with fresh straw and I noticed several large dogs lying on it under the tables, clearly waiting for scraps to be thrown to them. Everybody was dressed in silks and satins like us except for the servants who stood around the walls. The huge room was lit with many candles which flickered, their flames bending in the many draughts. It was a wonderful scene, festive and exciting.

Then the King entered and all the chattering and laughter died away. He was followed by a beautiful lady who I presumed was the Queen and four children who I identified at once by their various heights. Frisuthwith was the only girl. He noticed us at once and came over and asked if Edburga was treating us well. We said together, 'Yes, thank you, Your Majesty.' Then he said, 'Come with me,' and we followed him up to a long table set up at the end of the room almost under the musicians. We stood there, me on the King's right and Augie on his left, and the King surveyed his court. Then he said in a voice which carried to the far end, 'I wish to welcome two brave children to my court, June and August, who have travelled all the way from Jarrow with two valuable manuscripts from Father Bede for safekeeping here. I want them to be accorded every hospitality while they are here.' Almost the same words that Father Bede had used, I remembered. Then he said a short Grace but in English, not Latin, and finally he said, 'Now let us eat.'

Then everybody sat down and the food was served. Masses of meat but all deliciously cooked and many vegetables. I had the Queen next to me while we were eating and she asked me many questions about life in 'my country'. I was well rehearsed in my answers by now and she seemed satisfied with them. I noticed Augie talking to the King's oldest son who was sitting next to him on the other side of the King and hoped he was being as careful with his words as I was. At one point during the meal, which we ate mainly with our fingers, the King turned to me and said, 'Would you like to try some of York's famous mead?' I wasn't sure but finally shrugged and said, 'Sure. Why not?' So the King poured a little from his own cup directly into mine. I sipped cautiously. It burnt like honeyed fire going down and I gasped. The King laughed and said, 'Good, isn't it?' and then proceeded to give Augie some too. Realising it was the first alcohol I had ever tasted, I put my hand over the top of my cup to stop him giving me any more and promptly filled it up with water.

The musicians had been playing all the while and, although it was not easy to hear because of all the noise, I liked the music even though it was very different from the kind I was used to. Then, before the meal had finished, I saw Augie turn to the King, his cheeks flushed, and say, 'Would Your Majesty like us to play you some music from our country?' The King immediately agreed but then said, 'It seems, however, that you have no instruments with you.'

'It's in our room,' Augie said and, slipping away from the table, ran to get his recorder. I prayed that we weren't going to make fools of ourselves. He soon returned carrying it and the King called for quiet in the room. Then he said, 'Our two guests are now going to play some music for us from their country.' Augie started playing Old McDonald, rather hesitantly at first but soon getting into his stride, and I sang along with the recorder. The people in the dining hall all started tapping their feet in time with the rhythm and I realised they actually liked it. I wondered what they would say if we told them this was an old children's rhyme. When we finished, a great roar went up with everybody clapping and shouting for more. So we played and sang Ten Green Bottles and that seemed to go down even better. Augie finished by playing a short piece of Mozart he had learnt at school and the room fell completely silent during this. I wondered what they made of it but when he had finished, to another thunderous roar of approval, the king stood up and thanked us both for introducing them to some truly wondrous new music.

The meal ended with a sweet pudding which had honey in it and some unidentifiable spice. Then we were brought a bowl of warm water in which we washed our hands and given a cloth to dry them on. I was full again but not sleepy this time. In fact, I was buzzing with energy, probably from the excitement of the little concert we had given. I knew from the glitter in Augie's eyes that he felt the same as me. And, before we left the hall, he asked the King if we could play with his children for a bit. He said yes, of course we could, and we left with them and an elderly lady who was probably a nanny of some sort.

Chapter 14

We followed the nanny back to the children's quarters where we saw the baby who was feeding from a wetnurse. It was the first time I had seen this and I looked on curiously. He was a chubby little chap with red cheeks dressed in a silk nightgown and seemed to be enjoying the experience. He was sucking away voraciously and the wetnurse looked at me and gave me a big smile. She said, 'He's always hungry but he should be finished soon and then he'll go to sleep.' She switched to the other breast and the baby gave a few more big sucks and then closed his big blue eyes. The wetnurse unclamped him and slapped him lightly on the back. He burped and then fell asleep in the woman's arms. She carried him over to a big wooden crib and laid him down carefully in the satin sheets. I noticed that the room was warm and looked around for the source of the heat. Then I saw a fire burning away merrily behind the crib which had concealed it, the smoke disappearing up a chimney.

We left the baby's room and Frisuthwith invited me to go with her to her own room. I accepted her invitation eagerly, wanting to see how a princess lived, while Augie disappeared off to with Alcuin, presumably to his room. The nanny meanwhile had taken the two younger children to put them to bed.

We went up a flight of stairs to a door which had no special markings on it. Frisuthwith opened it and we went into her room. I looked around. So this was where an 8th century princess hung out, I thought. It was actually quite bare of furnishings. There was a big carved wooden chest which I assumed was for her clothes. In the middle of the room stood a small tapestry which was still being worked on and in the corner stood a musical instrument which I thought might be a lute. Her bed was richly carved and decorated with what looked like gold leaf and had a number of cloth dolls lying on it. There was a small table and a couple of chairs and that was it for furniture. It was lit by candles which were spluttering down to the end and I guessed that, when they finally went out, Frisuthwith would simply go to bed.

We sat on the chairs and she said, 'I like your voice. When you sang, it reminded me of birdsong.'

'Thank you,' I said. Then I pointed to the lute and asked, 'Could you play me something?'

'OK,' she replied and she picked up the lute and played what sounded like an old folk song. Then she started again and this time sang along with the lute. She had a clear, bright voice, even though it was untrained, and I sat there mesmerised. The song seemed to be about a great hero from the past called Beowulf who saved his people by killing a dragon.

When she had finished, I said, 'That was lovely. Thank you.'

'I wish I had a good singing teacher,' she said wistfully.

'But you have a lovely voice,' I said.

'Thank you but I'm worried in case my husband-to-be doesn't like it.'

'Are you due to be married soon?' I asked astonished.

'Yes, next year. My father has already chosen a husband for me.'

'Have you even met him?'

'No, not yet. I'm hoping he's not too ugly. Why were you surprised when I mentioned my future husband? After all, I **am** twelve, you know.'

'It's just that in my country girls, and boys too for that matter, don't usually get married until they are in their twenties, sometimes later.'

'Really? That's amazing! And do you get to choose who you're going to marry?'

'Yes, we do.'

'Oh, you are so lucky. I wish I lived in your country. Tell me more about it,' she commanded in a firm tone now.

'Maybe later. Can I see what you play with?' I said, changing the subject.

'I am not allowed to play proper games any longer,' Frisuthwith said sadly. 'I'll even have to get rid of my dolls when I get married. I just learn how to sew, play the lute and sing. Those are the accomplishments a lady has to learn here.'

I felt very sorry for her but, thinking of poor Alkelda, I said, 'But at least you have a loving family around you, don't you?'

'Yes, but not for much longer,' and she started to cry, a little girl's tears.

I put my arms around her and hugged her close to me. She hugged me back and slowly she calmed down. I said, 'I'm sorry if I made you cry.'

'Oh, it wasn't you. It was just everything.'

Then there was a tap on the door and the nanny came in and said, 'It's time for Frisuthwith to go to bed.'

'Goodnight, Frisuthwith,' I said. 'I hope I'll see you tomorrow.'

'Goodnight, June. I hope so too.'

And I left in search of Augie. I found him in Alcuin's room next door, admiring what looked like an entire arsenal of weapons laid out on Alcuin's bed.

Augie said excitedly, 'Alcuin has promised to show me how to fight properly.'

I was still thinking about poor Frisuthwith and had decided that I wouldn't like to be even a princess in this age and answered Augie distractedly, 'That's nice, Augie.'

He exploded. 'It's not just nice! It's brilliant!'

'I'm happy for you, Augie.' Then I turned to Alcuin and said, 'Please take it slowly with August. Remember he has no experience with weapons and I wouldn't like to have to take his dead body back to his parents in our country.'

'Yes, Miss June. I promise I'll look after your young friend. He will never be put in any danger.'

'Thank you, Alcuin. Now I think we should leave you and go to bed ourselves.'

'Yes, I am getting a bit sleepy now,' Augie said and he yawned. 'See you tomorrow, Alcuin.'

So we left and went back to our own room where we got ready for bed. Edburga came in and said, 'Did you have a good time with the Royal children?'

'It was interesting,' I said and Augie said, 'Alcuin is going to teach me how to fight!'

'It's important for a young man to learn that,' she said. 'It's time to go to sleep now. Good night.'

'Good night, Edburga,' we chorused.

When she had closed the shutters and left, I told Augie some of what Frisuthwith had said, especially about her forthcoming marriage, but he wasn't as shocked as I had been, saying merely that such things went on even in our own age. Then he started telling me all about the weapons I had seen but I fell asleep while he was still talking.

Chapter 15

We both slept well that night and had to be woken by Edburga who came in and noisily opened the shutters. She said, 'Come on, children. It's time to get up. The young master has to do battle with Alcuin and Frisuthwith has been asking for you, Lady June. But first breakfast.' We blearily washed our sleep-sodden faces and I said to Augie, 'I wish we had our toothbrushes and toothpaste with us.' Edburga heard this comment and disappeared for a couple of minutes saying, 'Wait here.' She came back, carrying what looked like two twigs taken from a tree. She said, 'Try these if you want to brush your teeth.' I looked at Augie but he just shrugged and took one. I took the other and put it in my mouth. It tasted vaguely sweet and I rubbed it between my teeth. When I had finished, I realised that my mouth felt much cleaner and I thanked Edburga saying, 'What kind of tree does this come from?' 'I'm not sure of the name,' she replied. 'But it comes from far away and we've been using it for generations.'

Then, when we were dressed, we followed her to the great kitchen which, like that in the monastery, was bustling with activity. She sat us down and we had breakfast. I felt much more awake now and asked Edburga where Frisuthwith was. 'In her room sewing probably,' she replied. So, while Augie went off 'to do battle' with Alcuin, I went up to her room and knocked. I heard her clear voice say, 'Come in'.

So I went in and saw her working on her tapestry. She came up to me and this time gave **me** a big hug. 'Good to see you, June,' she said. 'I just have to finish this bit and then we can go out. I want to see your horses.' So I sat and watched her deft little hands pulling the threads in and out of the material. I asked her what was going on in the picture, which looked like some kind of celebration. 'Oh, it's my marriage ceremony,' she said casually. 'It will form part of my dowry to my husband.' I confessed I wasn't sure what a dowry was and she explained that it was the money and things that a girl's father had to give the groom to thank him for taking her off his hands. I digested this idea slowly and then decided to say no more about it as I didn't want to upset her again by talking about her forthcoming marriage and, anyway, it was obviously the custom in this strange age. She snipped off a final piece of thread and said, 'There. It's the best I can do. I have never been very good at sewing.'

'You're miles better than me,' I said thoughtfully, looking at the picture with its gleaming colours and vividly realistic little people. Then I added, 'Edburga has offered to teach me how to do it.'

'She is famous in the palace for her tapestries,' Frisuthwith said. 'You are lucky to have her as a teacher. Come on now. Let's go out and see these famous horses of yours.'

So we left her room and went downstairs and outside into the courtyard. It was another lovely day and we saw Augie putting on some leather armour under Alcuin's directions. He had not bothered with any himself, knowing presumably that he didn't need it with a novice like Augie. I called out to him as we passed, 'Remember your promise, Alcuin.' 'I haven't forgotten, Miss June,' he called back and we went round to the back where the stables were. When we went in, Pegasus looked as if she had been waiting for me. She had her head erect and was looking at the door. When she saw me, she whinnied in greeting and I went up to her and patted her. Then I patted

Black Beauty and finally Northelm who was in the last stall. I turned back to look at Frisuthwith and saw her staring open-mouthed with astonishment.

'Are those really yours?' she breathed.

'Yes,' I replied simply.

'Where do they come from?' she asked.

'From my country,' I said.

'They are beautiful,' she said. And then she added, 'I bet my father would like them.'

And I thought back to what the King had said when he first saw the horses. 'Yes, I think he would,' I said.

'Can we ride them?' she then asked impetuously.

I was dubious about this idea and said, 'Well, mine is Pegasus and Augie's is Black Beauty. It depends on whether he'll let you. Ask him.'

She went up to Black Beauty and patted him and said, 'Will you let me ride you, master?' He looked at her and whinnied softly. He said, 'Yes,' she told me excitedly.

So I called the groom who was looking after them and asked him to saddle the horses. Then I remembered our clothes, our beautiful silk gowns, and asked Frisuthwith, 'How do we ride in clothes like these?'

'Oh, that's easy,' she replied. 'I'll show you.'

When they were saddled, I asked Pegasus to kneel so I could mount and both she and Black Beauty did so together. Frisuthwith looked on wonderingly at this sight but then the thought of riding a great horse like Black Beauty overcame the wonder and she jumped into the saddle, hiking up her dress unashamedly. I did the same and we were soon cantering away from the palace.

'We shouldn't go too far,' Frisuthwith said. 'My father will get cross.'

'OK. Race you to the trees over there,' I said, pointing to a wood in the distance.

Pegasus took off like a rocket with Black Beauty following close behind. We got to the trees in no time at all, the horses hardly working up a sweat, and Frisuthwith said, 'I haven't had so much fun for ages. I used to come here for picnics when I was little. There used to be a clearing in the middle. Let's see if it's still there.'

We proceeded slowly on through the wood, the horses stepping softly on the twigs and leaves under their hooves. Suddenly we came to a break in the trees and there in front of us was what must have been the clearing Frisuthwith knew from her childhood. But instead of being empty as we expected, it was full of fierce-looking men, most of whom seemed to be sharpening their weapons! 'Oh, no! Brigands!' Frisuthwith whispered. 'And so close to the palace!'

We started turning the horses to leave but the jingle of our harnesses must have given us away. The men looked up and saw us and the next thing we knew we were completely surrounded by them.

Their leader stepped forward and growled menacingly, 'You girls gave us quite a fright. Now tell me where you got these magnificent beasts,' and he came closer to Pegasus but she shied away. 'Oh, going to be difficult, are you?' he said, trying to grab Pegasus's bridle. Then he added, 'I'm afraid we're going to have to take them.'

Frisuthwith raised herself up in Black Beauty's saddle to her full, not very tall, height and said haughtily, 'Do you know who I am?'

The leader replied, 'I don't care if you're the Queen of Sheba. I want your horses.'

'I am the King's daughter,' Frisuthwith continued as if she hadn't heard him and I noticed some of the men step back looking worried. 'If you want to be hanged, you're going the right way about it.'

But the leader just said, 'Like I said, Miss, I don't care who you are. Just give us your horses and we'll let you go back to your Daddy.'

I bent down and whispered into Pegasus's ear, 'Let's go!' and with a mighty leap she soared right over the top of the astonished men, closely followed by Black Beauty. When we got through the wood, we galloped rapidly back to the palace with arrows raining down behind us but none could reach us. We were going too fast. We soon arrived back at the palace gates and trotted back to the stables.

As we dismounted, Frisuthwith said, 'Wow! That was close!' And patting Black Beauty, she added, 'You are truly a great horse.' He whinnied in reply as if to say, 'I know it but thank you anyway.' And then to me she said, 'I must go and tell my father to send some soldiers after the brigands.' And with those words she ran out of the stables.

I decided then to go and see how Wilbert was getting on and to tell him about my latest adventure. So, having given the horses a final pat and left them in the care of the groom, I left the stables myself and went to Wilbert's room. I found him out of bed and walking slowly up and down. He was obviously still a bit weak but getting better. He was eager for news and I told him what Augie was doing and about what had happened that morning to Frisuthwith and me. He told me that we had been lucky to escape, even with our amazing horses to help us, but I knew that already. He said finally that he should be able to join us soon and I said that we were both looking forward to that.

Then I left him to see if Augie had finished his battle with Alcuin. But, when I went into the courtyard, I saw him lying on the ground with his eyes closed and Alcuin standing over him with the tip of his sword pressed against his heart. I ran over and cried out, 'Is he dead?'

Augie, however, to my enormous relief, at once opened his eyes and jumped up saying, 'Of course I'm not dead, you dope. I was just pretending to be. It's a useful trick in a difficult situation, according to Alcuin.'

'You nearly gave me a heart attack!' I shouted angrily at him.

'But I'm fine. You can see that, can't you?' he said.

I calmed down then, knowing that I had over-reacted, and, looking at Alcuin, said, 'You may be able to use your fighting skills sooner than you think,

Alcuin. Your father is going to send a party of soldiers against a group of brigands camped near here.'

'How on earth do you know that?' he asked in astonishment.

'Never mind. I just do. Go and ask him yourself if you don't believe me.' I was still cross with them both for giving me such a shock.

'OK. I'll do that,' he said, giving me a curious look before leaving the courtyard.

'What have you been up to, June?' Augie asked.

So I repeated the whole story to him, much as I had told it to Wilbert.

'Ooh! It sounds exciting!' he said.

'It wasn't exciting. It was scary.' I said.

'Anyway, I've learnt a lot about fighting already,' he said, changing the subject.

'Good for you,' I said sarcastically.

'Let's go and find something to eat after I've got out of these things,' he said, taking off the leather helmet and body armour he was still wearing. 'All that fighting has made me hungry.'

'Again?' I said, even more sarcastically this time if that was possible, but he ignored my sarcasm.

So we left to find Edburga and ask about lunch.

Chapter 16

We found Edburga in her room still working on the same tapestry. 'How did the battle go?' she asked Augie.

'Well, I didn't win if that's what you mean,' he replied. 'But I learnt a lot.'

'Good. That's the important thing,' she said. And then turning to me she said, 'I hear you've been having adventures of your own, Lady June.'

I muttered something to the effect of 'I suppose so.'

'I also hear your horses saved your and Frisuthwith's lives,' she continued.

'Yes, that's true,' I said.

'Well, anyway, it's good to see you safe and sound.'

And then she led us down to the kitchen where we ate well. I found I too was hungry after the morning's excitement and I polished off everything on my plate. While we were finishing, another lady-in-waiting came up to Edburga and took her aside. When she came back, she looked grave.

'The King wants to see you at your earliest convenience,' she said.

'What about?' I asked.

'I don't know,' she said. 'But we have to go back to your room. You both have to bathe and get changed. You look like street urchins. And I have to do your hair again, Lady June.'

I looked down at my dress and realised it had patches of dirt on it and was very crumpled. Then I looked at Augie and noticed that he was even grubbier than me after rolling around in the courtyard all morning.

So we left the kitchen and went back to our room where Edburga ordered the servants to fill another bath and to bring some more clothes. By the time we had been bathed and changed and my, and even Augie's, reluctant hair had been brushed and we were looking respectable again, I noticed that the sky outside was getting darker.

'Is there a storm coming?' I asked Edburga.

She looked outside and said, 'Yes, it looks like it. Come on now. You're ready.'

So we trooped back to what I thought of as the King's study where he received us courteously and bade us sit. Then, looking at us both, he said, 'I have now had time to look at the manuscripts you brought me and they are truly wondrous in their different ways. I believe that Father Bede was right when he said that they should be kept safe for future generations to admire. So thank you both again for bringing them to me.'

We shifted restlessly in our chairs knowing that this was not why he had summoned us.

Then he looked at me and said, 'And I would like to thank you, June, for alerting me to the presence of the brigands. Alcuin has been dispatched with a contingent of my cavalry to deal with them. I should get word soon. Also I would like to thank you for saving my daughter's life.'

'It wasn't me. It was the horses,' I protested.

'Be that as it may, she told me that your quick thinking had a lot to do with it.' Then turning to Augie he said, 'And I would like to congratulate you, August, on acquitting yourself so creditably in your fight with my son. He told me he would be happy to have you fighting alongside him any time.'

Augie blushed with pleasure at the compliment but said nothing. We were both still waiting.

Then he continued more slowly, 'I have been in touch with the doctor tending to Wilbert and he told me that he should be fit to ride tomorrow. In his letter to me Father Bede asked me to return him as soon as possible. Apparently he's indispensable for his research. So I propose to send all three of you back tomorrow, accompanied by a troop of my cavalry to protect you on the way. I would, however, like you to give me something before you go.'

'As long as it's not our horses, we will give you whatever you want,' I burst out.

'That is exactly what I'd like,' he said. 'Is there nothing I could give you in return for them?' He was almost pleading now. 'I have jewels and many other valuables here.'

'No, I'm sorry,' I said. 'They're not for sale. We need them to get back to our own country.'

'Ah yes, this mythical country of yours where customs seem to be so different from ours,' he said pensively. I thought then that he might ask us some really difficult questions about where we came from which we couldn't answer but he just said regretfully, 'Oh well, I had to ask.'

'We really do need our horses,' I said and Augie backed me up by saying passionately, 'It's true. We couldn't do without them. We're sorry, Your Majesty.'

'Pity. But never mind. I promise I won't speak of it again,' the King said.

Just then there was a knock on the door and Alcuin burst in, flushed with excitement. He said, 'We've got the lot of them, Father. They were packing up their camp and managed to inflict a few scratches on my men but I'm sure none of them got away. A few of them unavoidably got killed.'

'Good. Well done, son. Throw them into the dungeons. I will deal with them soon.'

'Yes, Father.' And he left.

'One less problem,' the King murmured to himself. And I started to realise then what the burdens of kingship must involve. It made me think wistfully of my own relatively peaceful age and wonder if we would ever see it again.

'OK, children. I think we have covered everything. You may go now. I will see you at dinner.' We were dismissed.

We left him to his ruminations and went outside where we looked at each other.

'So we're being sent back to Jarrow, are we?' said Augie.

'It looks like it,' I said.

'Before I've completed my fighting education,' he wailed.

'And before I've learnt how to embroider. I think we might be reaching the end of our adventure, Augie,' I said.

'It's too soon! I like it here!' he said plaintively.

I thought he might burst into tears so I just said gently, 'I like it here too but remember your family, Augie.' That shut him up. Then I said, 'I'm going to find Frisuthwith to break the news to her.'

'OK. See you later. I want to find Alcuin to ask him about the battle with the brigands,' Augie said.

So we parted and I went up to Frisuthwith's room but she wasn't there. However, a maid was sweeping the floor and I asked her where she might be. 'I think she is with the Queen,' she replied. 'Where is her room?' I asked. She took me to a different part of the palace and pointed to a closed door. I thanked her and knocked diffidently.

'Come in,' said an imperious voice.

I went in and there was Frisuthwith showing her almost completed tapestry to the Queen. Her room was the most beautiful I had yet seen with gold and silver everywhere. There was jewellery laid out on a dressing table and many little bottles I guessed of perfume on it. It reminded me a bit of my mother's own messy dressing table although her jewellery wasn't nearly so magnificent.

'June,' Frisuthwith cried out and ran over and gave me one of her impulsive hugs. 'You look pretty,' she said and I replied, 'So do you, Frisuthwith.' And it was true. She had bathed and changed like me and looked radiant.

'I have some news,' I said seriously.

'Oh, what is it?' she asked anxiously.

'Your father is sending the three of us back to Jarrow tomorrow,' I said baldly, not knowing any other way to put it.

'Oh no!' she cried in desperation. 'You can't leave me yet! You've only just arrived!'

'I know. But it's not my decision,' I said. She looked thoroughly downcast and I hugged her back saying, 'You will always be in my thoughts, Frisuthwith.'

The Queen meanwhile had been watching this exchange in silence. But she broke in now saying, 'You know it's impossible to go against your father's wishes, Frisuthwith.' And then to me she said, 'I too will be sorry to see you leave, June. You are possibly the first real friend my daughter has ever had.'

I realised then that this was probably true but there was nothing I could say.

Then she said, 'But tonight we are having a big feast in honour of Alcuin being blooded in battle. So cheer up, you two. It's not tomorrow yet.'

Her mother's words put a smile on Frisuthwith's face and she said, 'Anything might happen before tomorrow.'

Then there was a tremendous crash of thunder which seemed to make the whole palace shake down to its very foundations and suddenly I heard the sound of rain cascading down outside.

'See?' said Frisuthwith triumphantly, 'I told you anything could happen. Perhaps the ground conditions will be too wet for you to leave tomorrow.'

'Perhaps,' I said doubtfully but then I decided she was right and I just had to make the most of this night.

The Queen then said, 'Would you like to borrow some of Frisuthwith's jewellery for tonight's feast, June?'

'I've never worn real jewellery,' I said wistfully.

'That's a great idea, Mummy,' Frisuthwith said enthusiastically. 'Come on. Let's go back to my room and you can try some on.'

'OK,' I said cheerfully, thinking that this should be yet another experience I could treasure for ever.

So back we went and Frisuthwith took her jewels out of a cupboard I hadn't noticed before in her room and we inspected them together. There was lots of gold and silver, beautifully woven into necklaces and bracelets inlaid with gleaming stones I didn't recognise, a few gorgeous rings, clearly designed for a child's finger, and a few other things. We tried some on me, Frisuthwith holding up a bronze mirror so I could see my reflection in the candlelight. She finally decided on a woven gold tiara which she said went well with my blonde hair and a simple silver necklace with a great blue stone hanging from it like a pendant. She clapped her hands when she had made her decision and said, 'Perfect. Now you look like a real princess.'

And I must say I felt like one.

She chose a couple of different items for herself and then said, 'It's nearly dinnertime. Let's go down and meet my parents.'

So we went back to the Queen's quarters where she was just having her long hair coiled up by a lady-in-waiting. She looked at me and said smiling, 'You are a beautiful child, June,' and I felt like a million dollars.

Soon she was ready and we went together to find the King. He was wearing the most sumptuous robe I had yet seen and he greeted us all warmly, giving me a peck on the cheek exactly as he did to Frisuthwith. Then we all went to find the boys. They were playing together, Augie and Alcuin in one corner of the room playing some sort of game with what looked like animal bones, Wicthed and Cuthbert in another being watched over by the vigilant nanny. Augie took one look at me and gasped, 'Crickey, June. You look good enough to eat.' I blushed and then followed the entire family down to the great dining hall with Augie taking up the rear.

Chapter 17

We had only gone a little way when there was a shout from behind us. 'Hey, wait for me, you guys!' It was Wilbert who was dressed in a fancy tunic like the other boys, beaming and looking the picture of health except for a large bandage still on his arm. He ran up to Augie and gave him a hug and then me. 'I've been given the all clear to leave my bed,' he said excitedly to the assembled group. 'And I understand that you are having a feast tonight in honour of Alcuin who I believe has saved the palace from a group of bandits. I'm hungry and with your permission, Your Majesty, I would like to join you,' he said, bowing to the King.

He laughed at Wilbert's impertinence and said, 'By all means, Wilbert. Do join us. It's good to see you looking so much better.' Then he introduced the Queen and the Royal children to him.

'It's great to meet you all,' Wilbert said. Then, turning to Alcuin the Younger, he said, 'I'm dying to hear about your exploits.'

'I understand you killed a great wolf to save August's and June's lives,' Alcuin said.

'I didn't do anything you wouldn't have done,' Wilbert said modestly.

Alcuin clapped him on the back and said, 'I like you, Wilbert. Sit next to me at dinner and we'll talk.' Then he noticed Augie looking jealously at Wilbert and added, 'And you of course young August can sit on my other side.' So with that problem diplomatically resolved, we proceeded on our way to the dining hall.

When we reached it, a great roar went up, everybody shouting, 'Alcuin! Alcuin!' He raised his arms in triumph and smiled at the assembly. I noticed the King looking proudly at his son. We went to our respective places at the high table, me sitting between the Queen and Frisuthwith, and Augie between the King and Alcuin with Wilbert on his other side. Then the King made a short speech about Alcuin's exploits and said Grace. The food was served and this time I was told it was venison or deer meat, as Frisuthwith explained to me. I had never had this and tried it cautiously but it was absolutely delicious. It came with some sort of gravy which was very rich but which supplemented its taste excellently. I chatted to Frisuthwith and tried not to eat too greedily but the Queen noticed me stuffing my face and said indulgently, 'It's good to see a child with a decent appetite.' Mead was flowing freely for the adults but the King thankfully didn't offer me any more and I stuck to water.

The meal finally ended and the King stood up and asked for silence. Then he said, 'I am sending our three young friends here back to Jarrow tomorrow. I would like to propose a toast for their speedy and safe arrival there.' And he raised his cup and everyone in the great hall did the same. I noticed Wilbert looking astonished at the news and realised that he couldn't have been told.

Then the King turned to us and said, 'You three need to get a decent night's sleep. You have a long journey ahead of you tomorrow.' So I kissed Frisuthwith and Augie and Wilbert hugged Alcuin and we all went our separate ways. Wilbert went back to his own room to sleep and we went to ours. It was still raining but not so hard now, I noticed.

The next morning dawned sunny and bright and I knew we would have to leave soon. So I took out the old sack of our modern clothes from its hiding place and transferred them to a silk bag which Edburga had kindly left us and which I knew would attract less attention.

Then I woke up Augie with a 'Come on, lazybones. It's time to get up.' He groaned and said, 'I think I ate too much last night.' But he was soon up and about. We went off to the kitchen to have breakfast which perked Augie up as I knew it would and then went to find Edburga. She was bustling around in our room packing things for us but, fortunately, without paying any attention to the silk bag into which I had stuffed our modern clothes. 'Good to see you up early,' she said but, when I looked closely, I could see tears in her eyes and realised that here was one more person who was going to miss us and us her. I hugged her and she kissed me as if I were her own child.

Then we went down to the courtyard which was full of soldiers with their horses, getting ready to leave with us. Most of the court seemed to be there also, including the entire Royal family. Frisuthwith came running up to me crying her eyes out and that made me start to cry also. We hugged each other tightly and she gave me the gold tiara I had worn the previous evening saying, 'I hope this will remind you of me,' and that made me cry even more. I popped it into the silk bag I had with me.

The king introduced us to the leader of our cavalry contingent, a polite young man called Gilbert and then Alcuin came over and said, 'I wish I could go with you guys but my father needs me here.' I looked around, through my tears, for Wilbert and then saw him leading Northelm into the courtyard. He waved at us and pointed behind him to where the groom was leading Pegasus and Black Beauty towards us. They looked as magnificent as ever and had their saddlebags back on. I slipped the silk bag into one of Pegasus's. The others I noticed were bulging, perhaps with food, I thought, or perhaps with presents for Father Bede.

Finally the King called the three of us to him and said, 'I would like to give you presents to thank you for bringing me the manuscripts and I think these might be the best things.' And he called Alcuin over who was admiring our horses. 'Alcuin, please present my gifts to our young friends,' he said. And Alcuin picked up a heavy-looking bag from the ground where he had left it and, to our amazement, took out three richly decorated weapons, a long sword for Wilbert, a short one for Augie and a dagger with a jewelled handle and a sharp-looking blade for me. The boys behaved like it was Christmas and oohed and aahed over their gifts. I, however, had no idea what to do with mine so I just curtsied to the King and put it in the same saddlebag as I had put our modern clothes. The King said, 'I hope you will be able to protect yourselves better with these weapons.' And we all thanked him while Augie and Wilbert put theirs proudly in their belts where they gleamed wickedly.

The King himself helped me up onto Pegasus and soon we were all ready to leave. We went through the big gate and, with a wave and a last sad look behind us, we were off across the plain. I still felt unhappy and I noticed that Augie did too. I assumed he too was thinking of the friends we had made at the palace.

We trotted with Northelm between us near the front of the column back the way we had come which seemed so long ago now. Then I asked Augie something I had forgotten about till now, 'What will happen to the prisoners?'

'Oh, Alcuin told me that the leaders will be executed and the rest sent packing without their weapons.'

'But that's barbaric!' I cried.

He just shrugged and said, 'It's the custom here,' and I realised then how far he was now a part of this age we had so easily stumbled into.

We chatted desultorily, feeling safe under the protection of the King's cavalry, and managed to make good progress across the plain. We stopped for lunch at a small village where everybody turned out to gape at us and then continued, making it almost to the base of the hills by nightfall. There we camped and Gilbert posted a ring of soldiers around us. We cooked our supper on some big fires which his men had built and which tasted like the barbeques I had had occasionally back at home. We slept on the ground which was uncomfortable for me at first but I soon got used to it and, under our warm blankets and in front of the fires, I actually slept very well.

Getting up at sunrise the next morning and having broken camp, we went on through the hills which we managed without incident. On the far side we came to the place where Wilbert had killed the wolf but there was nothing left of it except a skeleton. However, even that seemed to impress Gilbert. We continued onto the plain on the road to Jarrow when suddenly one of the scouts Gilbert had posted in front of us came galloping back and shouted, 'There are some huts burning ahead!' We squinted against the bright sunlight and saw that he was right. Far away we could just make out plumes of smoke rising into the air. Wilbert said angrily, 'It must be those wretched Norsemen we met on the way.' As we got closer, we saw that whoever it was had left a trail of devastation across the countryside. Whole fields had been burnt and the owners' huts left in smoking ruins.

We cantered up to Gilbert at the head of the column and told him of our suspicions. He said that we simply had to keep going on the same road as there was no other leading to Jarrow.

'What if they have got there already?' Wilbert asked anxiously.

'Then we'll have to do battle with them,' Gilbert replied grimly.

Augie was obviously feeling warlike for he said, 'I hope we do meet them. We'll give them a jolly good thrashing.'

I remembered the long column of Norsemen who had passed us while we were hidden in the trees and was dubious about that but it wasn't my place to speak. So we just kept going, all the while keeping a careful lookout for our enemies.

Chapter 18

As we got closer to Jarrow, we started to see whole villages burnt to the ground with young children sitting on the ground crying and no sign of their parents. I threw some food to them as we passed but we couldn't stop or do any more for them. A battle now seemed inevitable as we were clearly getting close to the barbarians. Then we saw a plume of dust in the distance approaching rapidly and one of the scouts came galloping back to say that a large group of heavily armed men were approaching.

The cavalry immediately surrounded us in a defensive ring while Gilbert sent a few of them off to a nearby clump of trees as reinforcements in case we were overwhelmed. He seemed to know his business as a cavalry leader, giving out his orders crisply and clearly. Then we just waited for what might happen. The cavalry men had all drawn their swords and I thought it would have been a beautiful sight had the circumstances been different.

The plume of dust quickly resolved itself into individual horsemen and I saw with dread the awesome figure of the Viking leader leading them. He came to within shouting distance of us and the rest of his men stopped and waited patiently. Then he shouted at us in Old Norse to surrender our weapons and our horses or we would all forfeit our lives. I translated what he had said to Gilbert who asked me to tell him that we would not surrender under any circumstances. I was by now utterly terrified but did as he had asked.

Then their fearsome leader roared, 'OK. So be it.' He drew his great battleaxe out of his belt, an obvious signal to his men that the battle was about to start. His men then drew out their own weapons and he gave the order to advance.

The next thing I heard was the ring of steel on steel. Everything became very confused but, when the Viking leader finally broke through our cavalry line, I thought that all was lost. He came charging right up to the three of us but Gilbert was there to defend us and soon he was fighting desperately. The noise of shouting men was terrific but I could see men on both sides losing limbs to the sharp steel which made me feel physically sick. It was nothing like the battles

I had so enjoyed watching on TV or in the cinema. This was real blood and it was much more horrible.

Then I noticed Augie say something to Wilbert and they both slipped off their horses. I called to them to stay with me but either they couldn't hear me in the din or they chose to ignore me. Wilbert went right up to the Viking leader waving his long sword and clearly issued a challenge to him for he roared with laughter and growled, 'So you want to fight me, do you, young whippersnapper?' Meanwhile I noticed Augie creep up behind him and, while he was distracted, suddenly lunge with his short sword straight between his shoulder blades. This time the leader roared with pain, not laughter, realising that he was now being attacked from three sides. He whirled round knocking Augie to the ground with his shield and then moved in for the kill. My heart was in my mouth but I could only look on with horrified fascination. Augie was lying there as if stunned but, as the Viking was bending over him preparing to strike the fatal blow, Augie suddenly raised his sword and plunged it this time right into his black heart. He gave a horrible gurgle, a trickle of blood came out of his mouth and he finally lay still.

All this had only taken a few seconds but Gilbert immediately came up and, taking the battleaxe the Viking had been wielding and raising it high above his head, shouted in his most commanding voice, 'Your leader is dead. You must surrender now.' A hush fell over the battle field and the enemy began to back away. Then Gilbert took some kind of horn out of his own bag and blew a great blast on it. This was the signal for the reinforcements hidden in the trees to attack. They came charging in and the Norsemen fled for their lives, dumping their weapons on the ground as they did so. It was a great victory.

Then we took stock of our own situation and found that, in fact, only four of our men had been seriously injured. They were patched up as best we could and put onto homemade stretchers, carried between two horses. The fallen enemy were left where they lay as food for the scavengers. Gilbert turned to us when our wounded had been seen to and said, 'We must hurry on to Jarrow now where we can get proper treatment for our injured men.' Then he turned to Augie and said, 'We owe you a great debt of gratitude, master August. Without your help we might well have been defeated.' Everybody clapped and cheered and I saw

Augie's chest swell with pride at these words but he just said, 'It was a trick Alcuin taught me.'

Pegasus and Black Beauty had been standing there stock still throughout the battle but, as soon as we were all mounted, they gave Northelm a nuzzle as if to say goodbye and galloped away very fast from the assembled men. We had no control whatever over them and could only go where they took us. I just had time to turn and wave to Wilbert and shout goodbye and we were out of earshot. I could guess where they were taking us.

Chapter 19

We had soon left our friends miles behind and were still galloping at the same breakneck pace through deserted countryside. No people, not a hut to be seen. Although we were riding next to each other, we had no chance to talk, all our strength being needed just to hold on. Then in the distance I saw a low hill with a large wood on top of it. I thought I recognised it and, taking one hand off the reins, I pointed it out to Augie. He nodded and we kept going. We soon arrived at the base of the hill and kept on swiftly until we reached the wood at the top where the horses finally slowed down. We made our way through the trees and, as I had suspected, arrived in the same clearing we had landed in all those days ago.

The horses knelt and we dismounted. Then Pegasus looked over her shoulder and I realised that she was looking directly at one of her saddlebags. I knew what I had to do so I took out the silk bag with our modern clothes in it and told Augie we had to change. We did so in silence and then got back on our horses again. The wood was completely quiet, not even any birdsong in it.

Then a great roaring began in our ears and we started to spin, faster and faster but forwards this time. Finally with a great leap, our magnificent steeds jumped into the void and we were spun so fast that everything became completely blurred and I had to close my eyes.

We landed as gently as leaves on the ground and, opening my eyes, I looked around. We were back on the carousel again which had now stopped spinning! Our magnificent horses had turned back into ones of glittering metal. We slipped off and ran to the entrance of the ride. We were the only ones to get off.

But, before we got there, Augie suddenly said, 'I just need to go back for a second,' and I knew that he wanted to rescue his precious recorder if he could. I remembered the gold tiara Frisuthwith had given me and ran back with him to see if we could find our treasures. But, when we got there, the horses' saddlebags, although still attached, were now also made of metal and welded shut. We gave them a last sad pat and I swear Pegasus winked at me.

Then we made our way to the entrance where the old clown was still sitting. I asked him what day it was. He didn't seem surprised by my question and replied, 'Why it's exactly the same day you came here. You've only been gone a few minutes.' There was a long pause while we digested this information and then he said, 'Did you have a good adventure? Don't forget, you only have to pay me if you did.'

'It was absolutely amazing,' Augie said. I wished there were some stronger words to convey our sense of wonder but just satisfied myself by pulling all the money I had with me out of my pocket and passing it to the old clown. Augie did the same and the clown thanked us and said, 'I'm glad you had a good time.' Then I asked him if we could come again. The clown laughed and said, 'Not this year but next year we should be passing through this town again. Try then.' And we had to be satisfied with that.

So we left him and the strange silence of the carousel and went through some kind of barrier into the noisy, exciting funfair. We didn't speak. There was too much to say. As we had no money left, we passed through the fair and walked back to our respective houses. Before we went in, however, I said to Augie, 'You know nobody will believe our adventure, don't you? I think it should remain our secret.' He agreed with me and we went in to join our respective families. My Mum asked me if I'd had a good time and I replied, 'Yes, wonderful, thanks,' and went up to my room where I decided to lie down. I fell asleep almost immediately and had some very confusing dreams. When I was called by my Mum downstairs for supper, I realised that my memory of the adventure was already starting to blur around the edges. That made me cross but there was nothing I could do about it. The next morning when I went to school, I whispered to Augie during break time, 'Do you remember much about our adventure?' He replied, 'No, it all seems to be disappearing fast.' 'For me too,' I said.

And within just a few days neither of us could remember anything at all about it except that we had certainly had one. We knew that for sure. And we couldn't wait for the next summer to roll round so we could visit the funfair again.

Epilogue

And I have been able to remember nothing until very recently when I had the chance to visit the British Library in London where I had to do some research for my history degree. I went into the mediaeval manuscripts section and there, staring me in the face, was the glorious original of the Lindisfarne Gospels. I was strangely drawn to it and, as I looked at its beautiful illustrations, the whole adventure suddenly came flooding back. I decided that this time I had to write it down and what you have just finished reading is the product of my memory. I have tried to get in touch with Augie so that he can check my manuscript for errors but have had no luck tracing him so far. I remember he moved back to America with his family after his school leaving exams when he was 16. Anyway, I dedicate this book to him and his bravery.

These days, when I am sitting at home alone, I often wonder what became of Father Bede (or the Venerable Bede as he is known today), and Wilbert,

Frisuthwith and all the others we met back in that time. Did Wilbert get back safely to the monastery? And, if he did, was the monastery still there or had it been sacked by the Vikings or the Pagans? And did Frisuthwith's marriage turn out happily in the end? But I know there's probably no way of finding out the answers to these and all my other questions.

Apart from the Gospels, there is, however, one other historical fact I know for sure. As soon as I returned from the British Library, my head still buzzing with the story I was about to write, I looked up on my computer the other manuscript we had carried from Jarrow to York, Father Bede's The History of the English Church and People. And, amazingly, it too has survived, and has been revered by scholars throughout the centuries as **the** major history of Anglo-Saxon Britain. So I knew that his book had been as important as he had said it was and our mission had been successful.

I think I had more adventures in later years but I guess I will just have to wait till something jogs my memory or the time is right.

The End

Lightning Source UK Ltd.
Milton Keynes UK
UKOW040854060313

207210UK00003B/234/P